A REALITY SHOW TO DIE FOR

COSTA RICA BEACH COZY MYSTERY SERIES #3

K.C. AMES

17th
STREET
BOOKS

AUTHOR'S NOTE

Hello and welcome!

If you love exotic animals, beaches, and good food then I'm pretty sure you're going to enjoy the fun ride ahead.

A Reality Show To Die For is the third book of my Costa Rica Beach Cozy Mystery Series.

There are many more adventures to come, so make sure you sign up for my newsletter so I can keep you in the know.

And by signing up you'll have access to a lot of cool stuff including my **Costa Rica Recipe Book**, free!

Subscribers will also have access to my personal pictures of some of the exotic animals I've encountered in Costa Rica (like sloths and monkeys) and pictures of my fearsome threesome (my Cavalier King Charles, Havanese, and Chihuahua).

https://kcames.com/subscribe/

ONE

The day that Hollywood came to the tiny beach town of Mariposa Beach in Costa Rica had started out like any other day at the Books, Bagels, and Lattes bookstore cafe.

As usual, the cafe got busy with the early-morning rush-hour crowd of caffeine-deprived and hungry locals and tourists, but by late morning the crowd dissipated until the lunch rush.

On that day, the sound of rumbling engines made the windows of the bookstore cafe rattle, disrupting the quiet. Dana Kirkpatrick and her friend and new business partner, Mindy Salas, looked at each other with wonderment in their eyes as they both rushed to the front window to look outside to see what was causing the noise.

They saw several large buses lumbering into town.

Mindy's husband, Leo, had also heard the noise, so he had popped his head from the back kitchen. "Oh boy, here we go," he said ominously.

"They're here," Mindy said, saying it like the little girl from the *Poltergeist* movie did.

Even Wally, Dana's shorthaired white cat and whom Dana

had anointed the official bookstore cat, had jumped up by the windowsill to watch the excitement unfolding outside.

"Wow, those buses are over the top," Dana said, looking at the large luxury buses pulling into town.

"It's the same buses that rock stars ride along in," Mindy said, sounding impressed as Amalfi Soto joined them at the window.

To Dana, they looked like two large, gaudy billboards on wheels. They had wrapped every inch of the buses with an advertisement for the hit reality television show, *The Island*.

The logo of the show was an island with palm trees and several stickmen in athletic poses like Olympians, and they had wrapped each bus entirely with the show's logo and the head-shot of the show's longtime host, Chris Day. His smiling face covered the entire center panels of the buses from the side flap to the roof—including the windows.

"Oh Lordy, that's one creepy man right there," Dana said, chuckling.

"That's the host of the show, he is so handsome." Mindy smiled wistfully as she spoke to Dana, but her gaze was on the bus.

"Hey, now," her husband said, pretending to be jealous.

Amalfi Soto, who worked for Dana, seemed in a trance looking out the window, and Dana didn't want to know what was going through her young nineteen-year-old mind because it was probably NSFW.

"That bus wrap is over the top, don't you think?" Dana asked.

"I think it looks cool," Amalfi said, focused on the scene outside.

"I think it's supposed to be over the top, silly," Mindy giggled.

Since they outnumbered Dana, she said nothing more, not wanting to be a Debbie Downer, since Mindy and Amalfi seemed to be fans of the show, Chris Day, and the bus decor.

Leo had already disappeared back into the kitchen.

Regardless of what she thought about the show or the buses, she was excited to have the beach town jam-packed with cast and crewmembers ready to spend money on books, coffee, and bagels.

Especially coming within the month since Dana and Mindy had combined their businesses—Dana's bookstore, and Mindy's cafe—under the same roof.

The idea to combine the businesses had come when Mindy's landlord saw how successful the cafe had become over the years, so he stuck her with a 300 percent rent increase. He figured she wouldn't want to move. He figured wrong.

Dana had bought her retail property for her bookstore outright versus renting in the heart of Mariposa Beach's tiny business district, known as Ark Row, across the street from Mindy's cafe.

One evening when Mindy was stressing out about what she would do about the exorbitant rent increase, Dana had an epiphany. "Move your cafe into my bookstore."

Dana remembered Mindy looking at her like she was off her rocker.

"I'm serious. I have a lot of room. I try as hard as I can, but my bookstore still looks scarce. And it's not like they're lining out the door to buy a book compared to the lines I see forming outside your cafe every day. You can have half of my retail space, which will be larger than what you have now. I'll even knock off some of your rent, and I promise I'll never be a pain in the rear landlord, nor would I ever try to gouge you with rent increases. We keep the business receipts separate. What you make from your cafe is all yours and what I make from the bookstore side is mine, so that stays the same, although you would miss out on the very lucrative bookstore business," Dana said, laughing.

Mindy laughed loudly at that.

"Okay, okay, not that funny," Dana said teasingly. "Besides, books, bagels, and coffee go together like peanut butter and jelly," Dana added, finishing her pitch.

After discussing it with her husband, who did most of the baking and managed the kitchen, and after they looked at the space to see if the move would be possible, Mindy and Leo agreed to combine the two businesses. Mariposa Books and Mindy's Coffee and Bagels became Mariposa Books, Bagels, and Lattes.

The move had gone smoothly, but there were a few days where they had to close, and the moving expenses for the Salas were a tad over budget, so the show coming to town was a boon to the entire local economy during the usual slowness of the wet season in Costa Rica, but it seemed like a lifeline to the new bookstore slash cafe, as Dana liked to refer to the new arrangement.

Besides, it wasn't every day that their sleepy little beach town got the Hollywood treatment.

After eleven seasons, the show was a big money earner for the studio, so they kept on cranking it out season after season.

In true Hollywood fashion, the network executives would squeeze every last drop of that moneymaking lemon until they sucked it dry and tossed what remained into the compost bin.

Dana had read that it was dirt cheap to produce reality TV compared to a network drama or sitcom.

The cast was made up of unknowns eager for a shot at fifteen minutes of fame and the one-million-dollar grand prize for the last person left on *The Island*.

The production company shot the shows on exotic islands in places like Costa Rica, Thailand, The Philippines, Indonesia, and other spots around the globe that were considered dirt cheap to shoot on location compared to the cost of shooting in LA.

It would be the second time they filmed a season in Costa Rica. Although Costa Rica was not an island, the country had several small, sparsely populated, rugged islands off both of its coasts.

The producers had chosen the tiny island of Santa Rita, which was located about twenty miles from the shores of Mariposa Beach, which was nestled right into the Nicoya Peninsula Bay.

The Nicoya Peninsula was the largest peninsula in the country and home to some of the most isolated and beautiful beaches, which made it a popular tourist destination.

Dana figured the fact that they had a pier that had served as the launching point to the island for decades had been a big reason why the producers chose their town to service as their headquarters while they shot the show.

It was a big production, with hundreds of producers and crewmembers arriving in August, which was one of the wettest months of the year, which meant that the jungle would be lush and green but everything would be wet and muddy from the daily rain and blasts of torrential downpours—a plus for the show's producers.

The tourist industry took a hit during the wet season, which is why it's considered the off-season for tourism. That also meant that the prices of just about everything went way down, and vacancies at the hotels and Airbnb were plentiful. Dana figured that was another reason the production company liked to film their show in August. Not only did the rainy weather make getting around more challenging, with muddy landslides, choppy waters, and with nonstop wet rain beating down on the cast members, it also made for much more compelling television to watch than blue skies and sunshine.

For the locals, it was a welcomed boost to the economy during its slow season, so they were more than happy to have the production team choose Mariposa Beach as their headquarters. It surprised Dana that the municipal mayor of Nicoya and his cronies weren't there rolling out the red carpet to welcome the production company.

Dana wasn't around when the reality show came to town five years earlier, but everyone who had been there told her they would pack her bookstore slash cafe with cast and crewmembers and that she should brace herself.

She had moved to the small, quirky beach town from the bustling and congested San Francisco a few months ago. It was a nice change of pace. It hadn't been a smooth move to town—far from it.

She had inherited her uncle's beach house, much to the chagrin of her cousin and his wife. Things got messy, really messy. There was a lawsuit and a murder—town gossip had her pegged as the probable killer. It was not a good introduction to the community.

Everything worked out with the lawsuit squashed, the murder solved, and the beach house known as Casa Verde and the acres of land it was on were all hers.

She had settled in nicely since then and had become a business owner for the first time in her life. And now there was the excitement of the show coming to town.

Mindy had been in business in town for over a decade, so she was here when *The Island* first came to town, and she had confirmed what Dana had heard from the locals that the production team was like money in the bank.

The town merchants of Ark Row called the production team walking ATMs.

"It will get crazy busy and we will make a lot of money," Mindy squealed. "But a warning," she said, her voice going from excited to ominous, "the crew is wonderful, but the cast can be a nightmare. A bunch of prima donna mactors."

"What the heck is a mactor?" Dana asked.

She had lived in LA and thought she knew the entire industry lingo. Mindy smiled and explained, "Model slash actors equals mactors."

"Oh, brother," Dana said, rolling her eyes.

"You'll see for yourself, half of them think they're the next great actor or actress, like they're a young Robert DeNiro or Meryl Streep, while the other half fancy themselves as super-models like Gisele Bündchen or Cindy Crawford."

Dana laughed at Mindy's descriptions.

"Did you forget I'm from California? I'm used to dealing with that kind of crazy. And although Northern California is more chill when it comes to Hollywood fakery, I lived for several years in Los Angeles, where dealing with plastic people like that was the norm."

Dana jostled her brown hair and made duck lips for added emphasis as Mindy and Amalfi cracked up.

As soon as the bus doors parted, open people began to pile out in droves. Most were young... very young.

Dana, Mindy, and Amalfi continued to watch as the chaotic scene outside unfolded when suddenly they saw several of them pointing towards their shop, and a horde of them began to make their way over. "Leo, incoming!" Mindy shouted over her shoulder towards the kitchen.

"Showtime," he shouted back.

"I'm ready for my close-up, Mr. DeMille," Dana said, and she and Mindy started laughing hysterically.

Amalfi looked confused, not getting the reference to the old movie, which made Dana and Mindy laugh even louder, feeling their age.

TWO

The Hollywood invaders razed through everything so fast that Mindy and her husband struggled to keep up with the orders. Dana and Amalfi manned the front, dealing with the victual demands of the barbarian hordes.

A few people perused the bookstore part of the café, but they did so while waiting for their food and coffee orders. So she was mostly helping Mindy keep up with the orders.

It should be cafe slash bookstore. Dana sighed to herself. *Oh, stop feeling sorry for yourself,* she soon chastised herself.

Amalfi Soto, who was the niece of Dana's property caretaker, had become a talented barista and a real pro. A whiz at making lattes, espressos, Americanos, mochas, and anything else that might be ordered. But lattes, teas, and straight up black coffee were the most popular items people ordered.

After fifteen minutes of nonstop customers, Dana looked up from behind the counter, and there were more people lining up. She blew a strand of brown hair away from her face.

"You guys weren't kidding about how busy we would get," Dana said between breaths.

There were always rumors that the reality show was coming back to town until they would read that they were going to another part of the world. The first confirmation that it was coming back to town was two months earlier, when a twenty-something-year-old assistant producer named Henry Robertson walked into the bookstore slash cafe to give them the spiel he had given to all the other business owners in Ark Row about how they were good for business and they wanted to be good neighbors and cause as little disruption as possible to their everyday life, yada, yada, yada. He seemed to be on autopilot by the time he made it to the bookstore slash cafe.

Dana knew that although assistant producer sounded like a fancy title, they were at the bottom rung of the production crew. They were the ones doing the grunt work that Henry was doing of going business to business then home to home giving the same spiel, over and over.

She had overheard Henry tell Amalfi, who had been flirting with the handsome young man, what he actually did when she asked if it was glamorous.

He scoffed. "Hardly. My official title is assistant line producer, and that just means I'm a glorified go-for at the beck and call of the line producer who manages the day-to-day activities of the set, which is why I get to do this and he doesn't," he said, sounding upset.

He spent the week before the production team arrived doing just that: going door to door like a political candidate, handing out a folder with the permanent information about the shooting schedule tucked in the folds inside which had all the information about their arrival and the strict rules of keeping away from the island during shooting.

Dana wondered how much that had cost them, to secure the island for themselves.

Dana had shrugged back then. "I don't have a boat, so that won't be a problem," she told him.

An hour after the crewmembers had descended into the cafe like a swarm of locusts on a farmer's crop, things quieted down again.

Dana, Mindy, Leo, and Amalfi could finally take a break.

"It takes a crew of about a hundred to film that show," Mindy said. "I think they all showed up just now."

"A hungry crew that downs coffee by the gallon and bagels by the metric ton. I wish they would film here every year," Leo added with a wide grin.

"I don't know about that, it was crazy busy," Dana said, having experienced the busiest day she had encountered at the cafe.

"Do you watch the show?" Leo asked Dana.

"Not really. I watched the first couple seasons then lost interest."

"I love it," Amalfi said.

It had been an interesting premise to Dana when the show first aired. The cast members were referred to as castaways; they were whisked away from the comforts of their first-world lives and were supposedly marooned on a deserted island. Each castaway competed against each other in a series of over-the-top challenges until the last man or woman left standing was declared the winner and awarded the grand prize of a cool one million bucks.

The runner-up won $100,000 dollars, and the third prize was worth $75,000 dollars.

All dozen castaways were paid $20,000 plus all their expenses for appearing on the show. Not a bad gig if you were willing to put up with the backstabbing, the elements, and grandstanding for the cameras.

Dana had loved the first season, and gave serious consideration into sending in her own audition tape for the second season but chickened out.

By the third season, the show had lost its luster for her. It was the same old, and the show was taken a much more drama-for-the-sake-of-drama approach, so she tuned out by mid-season and had watched none of the subsequent seasons.

She didn't even know that they had filmed in Costa Rica until the word spread through the small beach community that they were in the running for the upcoming season.

"I didn't even know they had filmed out here before," Dana said.

"Isla Santa Rita is right up their alley," Mindy explained.

"It's remote, with a choppy and rough boat ride to get there. And aside from a few marine biologists, the island is inhabited," Leo added.

"It used to be a prison, right?" Dana asked.

"Yes, but that was a long time ago. Back in the nineteenth century. The worst of the worst from all over Central America were dumped there to serve out their sentences," Mindy explained.

"Sounds like the book by Papillon," Dana said.

Leo shrugged and said, "Haven't read the book, but the movie with Steve McQueen and Dustin Hoffman was pretty good."

Mindy and Dana agreed.

"Wait, it was Charlie Hunnam and Rami Malek," Amalfi added, sounding confused.

"I feel so old, again," Dana said as everyone started to laugh.

"Anyway," Mindy said. "After ten or twenty years, they closed down the prison, and in the early twentieth century, it became a leper colony, but that closed down in the nineteen forties and it's been abandoned ever since. The old prison buildings are crumbling piles of concrete."

"What about the scientists on the island?" Dana asked.

"They're on the other side of the island, but they're usually not there during the rainy season as much, so the producers have the whole island for themselves."

"A penal colony then a leper colony, no wonder the producers love shooting there," Dana said.

"Well, I don't know how rough they have it in real life, since they're surrounded by a big crew including medics and nurses, but as you can see, it's good for business," Leo said, waving his arm at the empty coffee cups and plates.

"I even sold a few books," Dana said, smiling.

"Well, not everyone in town was happy about them coming into town," Mindy said.

Dana knew she meant the non-business-owning expats that had moved to town to live off the beaten path.

They eschewed the circus-like lives they left, only to have the circus move into their small, quiet town.

The older locals were not fans of the hoopla the production brought to town, either.

"A bunch of nonsense, if you ask me," eighty-one-year-old Doña Amada had told Dana a few weeks ago.

"They take over everything. Can't get a table at the Qué Vista restaurant or Oceanview or anywhere in town. And all those big, fancy trucks driving fast through town are annoying."

"Well, it's only for a month, and most of the time they're on the island anyway, so it's not a constant inconvenience. And I hate to say it, but they're great for business, especially during the off-season," Maria Rivera, the owner of the Qué Vista Restaurant, had told her.

As they were closing up for the day, Dana thought the

production people didn't seem as annoying as they had warned her.

"The people didn't seem that bad," Dana said.

"That was the crew. Wait till you run into the cast and the producers," Mindy warned.

Dana shrugged. *How bad could it be?* she thought.

THREE

After a busy day at the bookstore slash cafe, Dana was looking forward to relaxing in the evening.

They closed the shop at six p.m. and Dana hopped into Big Red. That was the nickname she had given the 1948 red Jeep Willys that she inherited from her uncle along with the beach house.

Her uncle loved that Jeep and had refurbished it a couple years before he died. After tooling around town and off-roading with Big Red the last few months, Dana understood why her uncle loved that little Jeep so much. It was a blast.

The first time she had laid eyes on the vehicle, she thought about Radar O'Reilly tooling around in those Army jeeps on M*A*S*H, just that her Jeep was painted cherry red, not army green.

But from the moment she fired the vehicle up, shifted into gear, and put her foot on the accelerator, she was a fan of Big Red.

The little Jeep was made for the ruggedness of the Nicoya Peninsula and the coastal beach towns of the Guanacaste Province and the Nosara District, where a lot of the roads weren't paved and those that were paved were littered with potholes the size of Texas.

That was why the most popular mode of transportation around town were Quad ATVs which Big Mike rented at his Surf Shop. He earned more from that than the business surfing brought in. Tourists loved riding around the beach in Quads.

Since it was the rainy season, Dana had the black vinyl soft top rolled up, but in the summer she loved buzzing around town without the soft top, feeling the mixture of the warm winds and the salty cool breezes off the Pacific Ocean in her hair and the hot sun kissing her face. Even though she had to take a mouthful of kicked-up dirt and dust from time to time, it was worth it.

She didn't have to worry about that today. It had rained hard in the morning but the water had dissipated by mid-afternoon, although the gray skies still hung around menacingly above, threatening to unleash another downpour. Dana was hoping Mother Nature was all bark and no bite so she could enjoy a dry evening.

As usual, it was pitch-dark out by the time she got home. The sun rose early in the tropics, by five thirty a.m., and went to bed early. By six p.m., darkness took over year-round.

The drive from the cafe to Casa Verde was just a few minutes long, which reminded her how much she did not miss the San Francisco Bay Area commute.

She got home and got out of her clothes, which smelled of old paperbacks, coffee, onion bagels, and cream cheese. She showered and dressed for dinner.

She was excited that Benny Campos was coming to town. Benny was an attorney in the capital city of San José.

In fact, that's how they met. He had been her uncle's attorney who handled all the legal paperwork and the boatload of problems that came to Dana when she inherited the property.

He was handsome and had the same brown eyes and hair color as Dana.

He was born and raised around the capital city of San José, but his family owned property near Mariposa Beach for decades, which he had inherited years ago. His beach home was on the other side of town from where Dana lived, but in the tiny town of Mariposa Beach, that meant a ten-minute drive from door to door.

Since there wasn't much business for an attorney in the tiny beach towns on the coast, Benny lived and worked in the capital.

He had a solo practice that specialized in real estate and immigration law catering to the expat community. Most of his clients were from abroad, the bulk from the United States and Canada.

At first, the relationship between Dana and Benny had been strictly professional even though a platonic friendship quickly developed.

That changed after a homicidal book collector tried to kill them both, an encounter that left Benny with a terrible concussion that took him months to recover from. He spent weeks in Mariposa Beach recovering, and the two of them became even closer until neither of them could keep their romantic feelings from each other.

The relationship evolved slowly and naturally, and she liked that. She had gone down the road of moving too fast in a relationship that eventually failed, so she figured it was time to try a different approach.

She didn't want to be like that fly that kept hurling itself against the same spot of the window over and over rather than move a little towards the open window.

They were both in their mid-thirties and divorced, and she

was finding dating was much less chaotic than in her early twenties.

There were other challenges. He had a nine-year-old daughter, which terrified Dana. She liked kids, but the idea of being the girlfriend of a tween's dad kept her up at night. But when Beatrice Campos had proven to be a darling young girl, she had put aside all the fears of the problem child.

The bigger challenge for her turned out to be the distance. It was difficult starting a new relationship with someone who lived over one hundred fifty miles away. The mostly two-lane highway system that was jam-packed with cars, buses, and semi-trucks meant being stuck behind an exhaust-spewing vehicle for four to five hours on a good day.

So their relationship was mostly via video chats on WhatsApp and on the weekends when he would come down. But Dana didn't want to think about any of that in that moment. He was on the way so they could enjoy a lovely dinner in town.

She checked her makeup, which she kept light. It was either too hot or too rainy for getting all gussied up in makeup, and besides she was living in the tropics now, where it wasn't practical and made her stand out from the locals.

She double-checked her choice of attire and she still approved of the knee-length navy blue free-flowing dress she was wearing. It was light, and she loved the deep front pockets so she could leave the purse at home. It was perfect for a nice dinner on the beach.

She was looking forward to a nice, quiet, and romantic dinner. Little did she know then what the night had in store for them, which would be anything but peaceful, quiet, or romantic.

FOUR

Dana and Benny were waiting for a table for almost ten minutes at the Qué Vista Restaurant—a rarity for Mariposa Beach, especially for regular and good-tipping diners like them who usually would get the Henry Hill from *Goodfellas* priority seating treatment.

Maria Rivera, the owner of the beach restaurant, saw them waiting and hurried over.

"Hi, guys, I'm sorry for the wait. It's these Hollywood people. It won't be long, I promise."

"It's okay, I'm loving the extra business myself," Dana said, smiling.

"It's nice, but some of these people, I tell you—" Maria was saying before a loud commotion coming from behind interrupted her.

Dana looked over Maria's shoulder towards the direction of a lot of yelling going on.

Maria turned around to witness the commotion, then she turned back towards Dana and Benny with an annoyed look on her face.

"See what I mean? Those two are on the show and they're

so drunk, especially the woman, so we refused to serve her anymore, so she yelled at us for a while and then they began yelling at each other. I thought they finally tired of yelling, but here we go, round three." Maria sounded exasperated.

"Who are they—" Dana began to ask, but was cut off by the sound of glass shattering on the floor, causing everyone in the restaurant to turn their heads towards the source of the chaos: the arguing couple.

Dana and Benny did the same thing as they craned their heads towards the back of the restaurant, where all the commotion was coming from.

"Oh jeez," Maria said with an exasperated expression as she took off towards the scene of the chaos.

Benny had caught the malfeasance in action when Dana and Maria were talking.

"She just threw a glass to the floor," he explained, amused.

"Oh, my," Dana said, craning her neck to get a better look.

Dana got the attention of Julio, the head waiter, and asked him who that was as she nodded in the chaos's direction.

"Cast members from that reality show," he replied with utter disdain.

The ruckus was happening at the back in one of the most popular tables in the restaurant, located on a wooden deck that was right on the berm of the beach, built on the white sand and within the swash zone of the Pacific Ocean mere feet away.

Besides the delicious food and the serene beauty of the ocean, dining right on the beach was the main calling card for the restaurant, where you could enjoy a great meal to the gentle sounds of the waves crashing on the shore nearby.

The rains had held up, so it was a beautiful night out with a comforting sea breeze, but Mother Nature's beauty and her generosity at holding back the rains couldn't compete for attention with the two loud drunks hurling glassware and insults at each other.

Even though Dana was far away from the action, she couldn't help but stare. It was like rubbernecking during a car accident. You don't want to do it. You know you shouldn't do it. But you do it anyway.

"Careful, you're going to strain your neck," Benny said teasingly.

Dana blushed. "Oh shush, I'm only human. I can't look away," she said as she continued to stare at the scene being caused by the good-looking couple.

It was becoming harder to ignore anyway, as they seemed to get louder and louder with every word spoken until they were just shouting at each other.

"No... no... no, I won't shut up! You shut up! You liar!" the female shouted, slurring her words.

"Bravo, as usual, you're making a scene!" the man shouted back.

"It's getting a bit ridiculous," Benny said. His voice had changed from amused to annoyed.

Dana watched as Maria and Julio walked up to the table of the battling cast mates.

She couldn't hear what Maria said, since she was speaking in her normal, calm, respectful voice, but Dana heard the female cast member's muttered response loudly.

"No, I won't keep it down! Do you know who I am? And where is my stupid drink? I'm dying of thirst over here."

To Dana, the woman's voice sounded like nails on a chalkboard.

Maria said something else, then an even louder outburst.

"I'm not going anywhere! I'll leave when I want to leave. You're not the boss of me."

Then she began to cuss Maria out with the vilest insults in

the book as her male companion sneered at her but did nothing to stop it.

"Enough is enough," Benny said as he made his way over towards the problem table.

"Benny, what are you doing..." Dana began to ask, but he was gone so fast that she was left standing there alone, so she followed him over to where the action was unfolding.

The inebriated and belligerent young woman saw Benny approach and she must have liked what she saw, because she gave him a drunken half smile. Her teeth were smeared in red lipstick, so it looked like she had been chewing on a magenta-colored crayon. Her black mascara had smeared. And although she was a beautiful woman, she looked like a character out of the *Rocky Horror Picture Show* at that moment.

"Well, hello, handsome," she slurred her words as she looked up at Benny from her table, batting her lashes at him. One of her fake eyelashes was barely hanging on for life.

Dana imagined the poor fake eyelash wanted to jump to escape the woman who was soused out of her head.

Benny was having none of that. He didn't suffer fools.

"Come on, they asked you to leave. It's time for you to go," Benny said firmly.

The drunken woman's dinner companion jumped from his seat, but he must have done that too quickly in his own drunken condition, because he swayed for a moment. Dana worried he would hurl, so she took two steps back.

The man finally regained his composure enough to glare at Benny.

"How dare you? This is Rose Budd, she's an Instagram influencer with one hundred thousand followers and is going to be the big star of this season of *The Island*. You can't talk to a celebrity that way!"

"Celebrity?" Dana scoffed. She put her hand over her mouth, not meaning to make things worse.

"She's an Instagram influencer," he said again, "what are you?" She felt his spittle land on her face and she recoiled in horror.

"Oh, gross! Say it, don't spray it!" she said back to him.

Rose Budd spoke up again, turning to face her dinner date, who was still standing and swaying. She stayed in her chair. "You've said worse things to me tonight, you jerk."

He looked at her then he kicked his chair to the ground and tossed a cloth napkin on the table. "Forget it then, just forget it. I've had it with you. It's over. I'm going to make your life miserable every day on that show, and I won't stop until you're voted off the island. You're a joke."

Before Benny could say or do anything, Rose got up, picked up a glass of water, and threw its contents right into the man's face. He flinched at feeling the cold water and ice cubes hit his face. He opened his mouth to say something but Rose Budd followed up by tossing the empty glass at him. It struck his chest and bounced to the floor, landing with a *thud*, but to Dana's amazement, it didn't break.

"Are you crazy?" the man yelled, rubbing his chest. He glared at Rose and said, seething, "You're going to regret that." The tone of the man's voice sent chills up Dana's spine, but he didn't seem to scare Rose.

"Oh, I'm so scared. You're just a wimp. I have more *cojones* than you," she yelled, and then she began to laugh in his face mockingly.

He stood there for a moment glaring at her and then he shifted his glare at Benny and finally he stormed off, shouting obscenities as he made his way through the restaurant and out its front door towards the parking lot.

"Go home and cry to your mommy, you jerk! I'll make sure

you don't even make it on to *The Island*. You're finished,
Robbie!" Rose screeched.

But Robbie was gone by then, so Rose plopped back down
on the chair. She was slouched down, looking disheveled.
"What a baby," she said under her breath.

She was breathing heavily. And then just like if she had
received a jolt of electricity into her body, she jerked up to her
feet and screamed, "Where is that vodka gimlet I ordered? The
service here is terrible. I'm a Yelp Elite Reviewer too, I'll crucify
you!"

"Out. That's it. And you're banned. Never come back here,"
Maria said, holding back tears.

It took Maria, Dana, Julio, and Benny to escort Rose Budd
from the restaurant.

And just like Robbie, she hurled obscenities the whole way
through the restaurant until they got her outside.

Once outside, they gently put her on a bench on the
beach, which Dana thought was very nice of them after her
loutish behavior and the horrible things she had been yelling
at them. If anyone deserved to be thrown out by the seat of
the pants onto the curb like in the movies, it was Rose
Budd.

"Don't come back to my restaurant ever again," Maria said,
her voice trembling from anger.

"Like I would want to choke down that vile trash you're
trying to pass for food at your crappy restaurant. I'm used to the
finest eating establishments in Los Angeles and New York
City," she said, slurring and now hiccupping.

Maria took a step towards Rose, but Dana gently put her
hand on her arm.

"She's not worth it, honey," Dana said.

"Besides, she probably won't remember a darn thing in the
morning," Benny said.

"I'll remember! And I'm a social media influencer and an Elite Yelper. I'll destroy your stupid restaurant," Rose cackled.

"So we've heard," Maria and Dana said, almost in unison. That cut the tension, and they all started laughing. Except for Rose Budd. She didn't laugh. She just slumped over to her side and passed out on the bench.

Just then, a black Range Rover pulled up behind them, its headlights shining brightly. A man in his early fifties with a George Hamilton tan and a Gordon Gekko haircut jumped out from the backseat.

"What's going on here? What are you doing to Rose?" he said in an accusatory tone.

Henry Robertson, the assistant producer, exited from the driver's side and stood behind the Gordon Gekko wannabe.

"Rose and her date Robbie made a scene at my restaurant. Breaking glasses. Hasn't even paid her tab. So I've kicked her out. She's lucky I don't call the police," Maria said.

The man's voice and demeanor quickly changed. "No need to call the police. So sorry about that. I'm Russ Donnelly. I'm the Creator and Executive Producer of *The Island*. Rose Budd and Robbie Gibbons are part of this year's cast. I'll make sure they won't cause any more problems in this beautiful little town," he said with a bit of condescension as he flashed a car salesman smile with teeth that were too bright to be natural.

Donnelly then reached into his pants pocket, pulling out a wad of bills. He peeled off three one-hundred-dollar bills, and he proffered them in the air, saying, "This should cover the bill and any damages incurred." His manner and voice were even more condescending than before.

Dana watched Maria hesitate taking the money, so she yanked the cash from Donnelly's hand and gave it to Maria.

"Covers some of the damages, at least," Dana said. Donnelly looked at her, confused.

Maria smiled then said, "One more thing. I don't want those two lunatics back at my restaurant. We told them they're banned, but in case they don't remember that once they sober up, please let them know they're not welcome back."

"They're also banned from Books, Bagels, and Lattes," Dana added for good measure.

"Absolutely. We shoot in a few days anyway, and tomorrow, Rose and the rest of the cast and crew will be on the island and out of your hair until we wrap up shooting in a few weeks."

Donnelly looked over at the bench where Rose was snoring loudly, her short skirt revealing way too much. Donnelly's face turned to stone as he glowered at her. "Her antics are wearing me thin," he said under his breath as he shook his head. He nodded at Henry, who then tried to wake her up. When that failed, he picked her up in a fireman's carry and dumped her into the backseat of the Range Rover.

"Good night," Donnelly said as he climbed into the vehicle.

The car took off, and Dana just stood there with everyone else for a moment in shock.

FIVE

The next morning, Dana went for a run. She liked to go in the morning when the temperatures were cooler and most of the town was asleep.

She got dressed in her running shirt and shorts. She laced up her light blue ASICS running shoes. She loaded up an audiobook on her phone. It was the latest *Rizzoli & Isles* novel by Tess Gerritsen.

"You want to come for a run?" Dana teased her cat, Wally, who yawned and gave her a dirty look.

She went outside, and it was a crisp and cool morning, but there was a tinge of humidity in the air already, so it would be another hot day in the tropics. She looked up at the gray sky, but Mother Nature was holding back the rain for now.

She exited her property through a side gate that spilled out into a pedestrian footpath that led down to the beach.

Her routine was to walk briskly down the footpath through the woods that spilled out right onto Main Street. It took just a few minutes, but it was a good way to loosen up. From there, she would begin her run. She ran past Ark Row. All the retail stores were closed, including her own, although Mindy and Leo would soon arrive to prepare for the early-morning rush.

She hadn't gotten too far when she noticed a bevy of activity down by the pier and the only boat landing stage in town, so she stopped to look at the throng of people and equipment out on the pier.

The pier's platform and pillars that led out from the shore into the ocean were made from wood. Dana always thought it looked too weatherworn and rickety for her comfort level.

Since it was Mariposa Beach's only pier, it had been aptly named Muelle Uno. The Spanish moniker for the pier—Muelle Uno—didn't get a rise from most people, but its English translation, Pier One, did. Amused tourists would giggle and ask if the Pier One of Mariposa Beach carried wicker ottomans and bowl-shaped chairs.

The locals had heard the same joke so many times that many of them would roll their eyes and reply with some variation that all they had to do was to walk towards the end of the pier until they hit the water and they would find the retail store down there underwater.

It was the favorite comeback to the question about Pier One sales of Gerónimo Díaz, the old, crusty, self-appointed pier master.

The landing stage for boats was small, allowing two boats to dock there at one time.

Pier One was mostly used by Don Gerónimo, a tico—a Costa Rican—and Bill Kingman, an expat from the Florida Gulf Coast who moved to Mariposa Beach six years ago.

They were the only professional captains in town who took out tourists on deep-sea fishing trips, whale watching, or leisure sunset boat rides in their catamarans.

Dana stopped and watched at the mayhem down below. It

looked like the production company had hired both captains to ferry the cast and crew to the island. And from the look of all the gear lined up on the pier, they were going to haul a ton of equipment too.

Dana shuddered, thinking about all that weight on that flimsy pier, but smiled, thinking how thrilled Don Gerónimo and Bill were about the steady work being provided by the production company during the slow tourist season.

Dana was taking it all when she saw Big Mike mingling with the Hollywood invaders.

She called out his name. He looked up, spotting her, and smiled and waved at her as he made his way towards where she was standing.

Big Mike was one of the Ark Row merchants, the owner of Big Mike's Surf Shop. He was a former professional surfer who was born and raised not in California, Hawaii, or Australia like one expects a professional surfer to be from, but from the doubly landlocked state of Kansas, where Oklahoma and Texas stood in his way to the Gulf of Mexico. Not that it stopped him from becoming a professional surfer.

Big Mike's real name was Mike Pavlopoulos. He was about five feet six and scrawny, so Dana—just like probably everyone else that first met him—wondered why his nickname was Big Mike. She had learned when she first met him that he got that nickname for surfing the big waves like at Mavericks in Half Moon Bay, California, not because of his physical appearance; if his nickname were based on that, it would be Little Mike, not Big Mike.

"Hey, girl," he said, sporting a big smile as he walked on over to where she was watching the mayhem unfold.

He was in his forties. His skin was tanned and leathery looking from decades of living on the beach—a reminder for Dana that she needed to be applying the right sunscreen and stop forgetting her wide-rim hat at home when she was out and about in the tropics.

"What are you doing down there with the production crew?" she asked, feeling a bit embarrassed for being so snoopy. *You're dangerously close to becoming an honorary member of the Gossip Brigade*, she thought.

"Oh, I got a job. It's pretty groovy," he said, smiling. As usual, he flashed a Hawaiian hang ten hand gesture at the same time.

"It's a one-month contract as a technical advisor for the show. I'll help them out with the waters out here and I'll be helping them design some of the challenges for the show. It's wild stuff. But I can't say much more than that, since I signed a thick non-disclosure agreement," Big Mike said as he put his index finger to his lips and hissed *shh*.

"What about your store?"

"Carlitos and Connie can hold the fort down for me. Besides, this is just a part-time gig, so I'll be at the store most days when I'm not needed on the island."

Carlitos and Connie were surfing cousins that worked for Big Mike.

"Well, that sounds cool. I can't wait to watch the show now that I know it's being shot here and that you're involved with coming up with those challenges."

"Yeah, I will make the beautiful people on the cast want to run back to Mommy and Daddy after going through one of my creations," Big Mike said with a sly grin.

"We'll have to plan a viewing party when it airs," Dana said excitedly.

"That would be awesome. Well, I have to boogie. Later, Dana," Big Mike said, flashing another hang ten hand gesture as he turned to head back towards the pier.

"Have fun," she said, waving at him.

She felt like a sailor's woman sending off her man to sea. She shuddered at the thought of her and Big Mike as anything more than good friends and business neighbors.

She watched for a moment longer and was just about to get to that run when she heard Doña Amada's high-pitched shrilly voice from behind. "What a bunch of nonsense."

Dana turned to face Doña Amada and Doña Chilla, two of the four old ladies that made up Mariposa Beach's infamous Gossip Brigade.

"All that hoopla over a stupid show?" Doña Amada said, sounding miffed.

"Oh, hush, Amada," Doña Chilla said, surprising Dana, since she rarely stood up to the de facto leader of the group. "I think it's wonderful. It brings a little of that Hollywood glamor to our little beach town, and it's great for the local businesses, isn't that right, Dana?" Doña Chilla said, looking down towards the hubbub at the pier.

She was always the sweet and positive one of the Gossip Brigade, Dana thought. "You're right, it's great for business. A godsend during the slow wet season."

Doña Amada scoffed even louder, and Dana could have sworn she heard her snort. "Hollywood glamor? Please. It's not like it's Tony Curtis and Marilyn Monroe down there, just a bunch of wild youngsters eager to make fools of themselves for a few minutes of TV fame."

Doña Amada had a well-deserved reputation for being the town's loudmouth. She was a crusty, feisty, and ill-tempered curmudgeon, but Dana agreed with the firecracker octogenarian about her assessment of the cast for these types of reality shows.

She also knew these old biddies loved to fight and argue with each other so she decided she would head out before their latest verbal wrestling match went to the mat.

"Okay, ladies, I'm going on my run. Have fun," Dana said.

Both ladies barely acknowledged her as she took off.

"You're crazy, how can you say that, look at all that over there, it's a touch of Hollywood, right here in our little town."

"Oh, please, a touch of Hollywood trash, if you ask me."

"I didn't ask you—" was the last Dana heard as she put her ear buds in and began running once again, chuckling.

SIX

It had been two days since Dana saw the cast and crew gathering around Pier One. And just as Russ Donnelly had promised that night at the restaurant, the cast and crew had left Mariposa Beach to the island and things quickly quieted down and got back to normal in town.

As a resident, Dana welcomed the peace and quiet. As a business owner, she missed the uptick in business the production company brought to her bookstore slash coffee shop.

Dana woke up to the sound of loud purring. She opened her eyes and her cat was sitting on her chest, staring at her.

"What do you want?" she said, yawning.

The cat stretched and went into downward dog yoga pose right on her chest. "Hey, I'm not your yoga mat." Dana laughed. Wally licked his lips and yawned again.

"I guess it's time to get up, huh Wally?"

He meowed. Dana assumed that meant yes.

She got out of bed, fed Wally, and got into her running clothes.

She hadn't gone out since the last couple days, and that run had been cut short when she became distracted with the Holly-

wood invaders getting into the catamarans to head out to Santa
Rita Island.

So she planned to run longer on that morning. She had her
running routes down to a T. The longish one had her running
out her back door and up the footpath up the mountain towards
the Tranquil Bay Resort, which was located about a mile up the
mountain.

Gustavo Barca was the bigwig rich guy in town who owned
the five-star resort. The footpath led from Casa Verde past a
yoga retreat, a bed and breakfast, and then up to the resort.

In the other direction, the footpath led the resort's hoity-
toity guests from their posh accommodations down to the local
retail stores in town and onto the beautiful white-sand beaches
and the warm, calm waters of Mariposa Beach.

Barca made sure the footpath was well maintained and
clear, which was great for Dana, since it was officially on public
land, so anyone could use it, much to Barca's chagrin. He
wanted the footpath to be used only by his guests. He tried to
make that happen by filing a lawsuit against the town, but a
Costa Rican court had disagreed with him and the footpath
remained open to the public at large.

Dana ran up the footpath past the resort and onto the paved
freeway, which she would then run on all the way back to town
and then back to Casa Verde.

She also had her I'm-in-a-hurry route, which had her
running out her front gate down to Main Street and through
Mariposa Beach, where she would run about a mile out of town
before turning back.

Then there was the I-have-the-time beach route, which had
her running out her front door down to the beach, about half a
mile through town, then she would run on the beach for two
miles, avoiding the crashing waves from gobbling up her expensive running shoes, although it was usually inevitable that the

Pacific Ocean wouldn't have its fun in getting her running shoes wet anyway by unleashing a sneaky wave or two her way.

She would run on the shoreline until she hit the eroded limestone rocks that divided Mariposa Beach and Cielo Lindo Beach, which was the neighboring town to the south.

At that point she would turn back and run back towards Mariposa Beach and then she would finish by walking the last half a mile from the beach to her house. It was a good five miles in total, and it had been a few weeks since she had run that route, so she settled on it.

She slipped her mobile phone into a plastic protective pouch that was attached to an armband, which Dana slipped over her right arm. She plopped the white ear buds into her ears and continued listening to her audiobook.

She walked out her front door, waving at Ramón, her groundskeeper and property caretaker, who was chopping up yuca with a machete at seven o'clock in the morning.

She walked out her front gate and down the gravel road that connected to the palm-tree-lined Main Street past the trees favored by the howler monkeys that loved keeping her up at night. She waved at the monkeys, running out of the woods, past Ark Row and towards the Qué Vista Restaurant, which was closed, but she saw Julio, the head waiter and manager of the restaurant, and a delivery man who was unloading supplies from a semitruck that made weekly deliveries from San José.

She waved at them too as she ran past them.

She noticed the deliveryman ogling her, making her feel creeped out. She glanced over again, and she saw Julio give him a shove as if to tell him to knock it off. It made her smile.

He's such a sweetheart, she thought.

She picked up the pace once she hit the beach.

Her feet sank into the loose sand from the berm, so she

trudged down towards the shoreline where the high tide had left soft, dry sand to run on.

Dana ran until making it to the rocks, where she stopped to capture her breath and take in the view.

She looked around the mountainous peninsula with its heavily forested hillside to her right and the mountain ranges known as the Cordillera de Guanacaste off in the distance, lush green from all the rains. And directly in front, the vastness of the Pacific Ocean that would go on and on for thousands and thousands of miles towards Hawaii, eventually reaching southeast Asia. The world seemed so beautiful standing there that you could forget bad stuff could happen anywhere, even here.

She checked her time. Her run was turning into a nature hike. She removed her ear buds to listen to the lovely sounds of the waves crashing into the rocks. The wind was whistling, and she could hear a laughing gull out there somewhere.

She was about to head back when her attention was directed to something that had washed up against the rocks.

Oh, great, more trash washing up from who knows where, she thought, annoyed. Every month, a bunch of the townspeople hit the beach to pick up trash from the shoreline. It worried her that the trash would be swept back into the water, so she looked around and picked up a piece of driftwood so she could pluck the garbage from the rocks before the tides took it back out to sea.

Her plan was to get it as far away from the waves so she could come pick it up later to throw it away.

She walked up to the edge of the rocks with a piece of driftwood in her right hand. She climbed a large rock as a wave splashed water on her face. It felt good and cooling to her sweaty skin. She could taste the sea salt on her lips.

She looked down at the debris and flinched. *It can't be.*

She got a little closer and the piece of driftwood that was in her hand fell onto the rocks below, but she didn't even notice; she was transfixed looking at a body jutting out of the rocks as waves kept washing over it. The body swayed gently in a puddle of water left on the rocks by the waves.

She wanted to look away, but she was incredulous about what she was seeing, then she saw blonde hair floating around the head like moss in the water. That's when she saw an arm twisted in a way that wasn't natural, and still her brain tried to talk her out of what she was seeing.

No, that's not a human body, silly. Until finally the cerebral cortex part of her brain took over and yelled at her, *Yes, that is a body. Now, RUN!*

She did as her brain told her and took off running away so fast that she almost stumbled and fell, but she recovered. Her body unleashed an adrenaline surge that she swore would have caused her to overtake Usain Bolt at that moment.

She ran up to the paved road, but she didn't see any vehicles, so she kept running until she got back to Mariposa Beach, out of breath and heaving heavily.

She made her way back to the Qué Vista, where Julio and the deliveryman were still unloading the truck.

"Wow, that must have been some run," Julio said, looking at her sweating profusely, panting, and her body trembling. It wasn't until that instant that she remembered she had her mobile phone with her the whole time, so she could have called for help, but in her panic she ran straight into town at full speed. She was spent, bending at her knees, trying to catch her breath while trying to tell Julio what she saw.

Between deep gasps for air, she said, wheezing, "Call... police... dead.. body... on... the... beach... rocks."

SEVEN

In the few months that Dana had been living in Mariposa Beach, she had noticed that the police presence in rural Costa Rica was sparse, and that was being very kind.

The town was in the Nosara District, which was part of the Guanacaste Province. Unlike the United States and other countries where most towns had their own police force, Costa Rica had a national police force, the Fuerza Pública—Public Force—which was under the Ministry of Public Security.

The Public Force operated on a geographic command basis not down to the town level, so they had a much larger ground to cover than a typical city police department or a sheriff's department working at the county level back in the States.

But like a city police department in the United States, the police officers of the Public Force handled the day-to-day law enforcement duties on the ground like providing security, law enforcement, protecting citizens, etc.

The closest police presence to Mariposa Beach was a tiny substation in the town of Guiones Beach that was about twice as large as Mariposa Beach and about twenty miles away.

Since there were many more hotels and resorts in the coastal area of the Nosara District and tourists flocked to the district like moths to a light bulb, the substation in Playa Guiones was part of the Tourist Police Unit.

The National Public Force was divided to serve the different law enforcement needs of the country such as traffic control, vice, and narcotics, and since tourism was the bread and butter to the economy of the country—especially on the coast—the Public Force had a dedicated squad of police officers to serve and protect tourists.

The substation was staffed by a handful of police officers with the Tourist Unit that zipped up and down the coast in motocross bikes.

Because of the twenty-mile distance between Guiones Beach and Mariposa Beach, it would take around twenty to thirty minutes for them to make their way down to Mariposa Beach, longer if it was a busy day.

Complicating things, in Costa Rica, the National Police couldn't investigate crimes or charge suspects with crimes. Only the elite Judicial Investigative Police—known by its Spanish initials for Organismo de Investigación Judicial: OIJ—could do that.

Its agents were a cross between a police detective in a department like the NYPD or the LAPD and an FBI agent.

The closest OIJ station was almost fifty miles away in Nicoya. So the tourist police officer from Guiones Beach would arrive to secure the scene and provide a modicum of security for the residents as word began to spread through town that Dana had found a dead body. But then everyone had to wait until the detectives who could investigate crimes arrived from Nicoya.

Officer Freddy Sanchez was one of the police officers in the Tourist Squad that were assigned to cover a large swath of area from Guiones Beach down to Samara and everything in between, which included Mariposa Beach.

Twenty-six minutes after Julio had called the police, Officer Freddy Sanchez came roaring down Main Street on his Honda motorcycle with its blue siren flashing. *Pretty quick response time around these parts,* Dana thought.

He came in fast, leaning into the motocross bike sideways like he was riding in the Motorcycle Grand Prix. He slid the bike into a full stop in front of the Que Vista restaurant, kicking up dust and dirt.

He got off his white and blue motorcycle and removed his helmet and replaced it with a baseball hat with the word POLICIA emblazoned on the front of the cap. He wore black pants and a white short-sleeve polo shirt with "Policía Turista"— Tourist Police—emblazoned on the back of his shirt and the Public Force emblem embroidered on his breast pocket. It was the uniform of the Tourist Police.

"Where's the body?" he asked, looking around as if he were expecting to find it lying somewhere near the restaurant.

"It's a couple miles from here. Over by the rocks," a shaken Dana replied.

She had recovered from the mad dash to the restaurant and was now speaking normally thanks to the two bottles of water Julio had given her to calm her nerves and clear her parched throat.

Benny arrived in his SUV a minute later. Dana had forgotten she had texted him but was relieved to see him pull up.

"Are you all right?" he asked, putting his arm around her.

"I'm fine. But there is someone over by the rocks on the beach that is not."

"Let's go over there so you can show me the body," Officer Freddy ordered.

"I'll drive you," Benny said.

"I'll follow you," Officer Freddy said, jumping back on his motocross bike and starting it.

Dana climbed onto the passenger side and shivered from the blast of the air conditioner from Benny's SUV.

"Are you really okay?"

Dana nodded. "Unfortunately, it's not my first rodeo in the finding a dead body arena."

It had been a few months since Dana had found the dead body of the local eccentric, Barry Shy, in her bookstore coffee shop days before its grand opening.

"Oh, boy, I think the word has reached the Gossip Brigade. Doña Amada is heading our way."

"Ugh," Dana said, watching the gossipy old lady making her way over spryly towards the SUV, waving her hands in the air.

Benny and Dana waved at her, playing dumb as Benny tossed the SUV into gear and pulled out from the restaurant's parking lot and down to the beach, leaving the old lady standing there with her arms on both hips.

"You will have to pay for that," Dana said with a laugh.

Benny drove down the road and then onto the actual beach, Officer Freddy following him. He had to maneuver the SUV carefully on the soft sand until the tires hit the hard sand of the splash zone and he sped down towards the rock formation, which was the town limit of Mariposa Beach.

Officer Freddy zoomed past him on his dirt bike, unable to resist the urge to pop a wheelie as he zoomed towards the rocks.

"He must have figured out the spot," Dana said, watching him speed away.

"It's a small town. Everyone knows where the rocks are," Benny explained.

It only took a couple minutes to get there. Officer Freddy had already gotten off his bike as Benny parked on the beach right behind the motorcycle.

"Over there?" the cop asked, pointing towards the rocks.

"Yes," Dana said. She began to tremble again, picturing the body in her head.

"I don't want to go over there again, but if you go up and over those rocks, you'll see the body down there."

"I understand. I'll be right back," Officer Freddy said as he removed a roll of yellow police tape from his bike's side pouch. He headed over to the rocks and climbed onto a large boulder that was wet from the waves crashing into it. He climbed up the rocks carefully. Dana figured he wanted to make sure not to disturb the crime scene and not to slip on the slick rocks.

After a few seconds, she heard him shout out, "I see it."

Dana could see him standing on top of the boulder. He looked around carefully before he dropped to the other side of the rocks where he was no longer visible to Dana and Benny.

They stood there for a few minutes, giving each other confused glances before Officer Freddy popped back up from the other side of the rocks with a trail of yellow tape that he continued crisscrossing until he had cordoned off the area.

EIGHT

Dana and Benny waited for about ten minutes as Officer Freddy did whatever police work he had to do in order to secure the scene for the detectives, who were on their way from Nicoya.

Dana had been under the notion that the poor woman ended up dead because of some accident. Drowning always took its share of tourists and locals around the coast.

The skies darkened, and the temperature dropped. Dana looked up, and she felt a few raindrops hit her face and arms gently. It was as if Mother Nature was giving her a little nudge of warning to go for cover because she was getting ready to open up the floodgates from above.

Officer Freddy sauntered back to where Dana and Benny were standing, holding each other in an embrace, but really it was Benny who had wrapped up Dana into his arms.

Officer Freddy looked up at the sky, worried. He knew what Mother Nature was about to deliver.

Dana had watched enough true crime shows to know that rain is a crime scene's worst enemy. But then again, she thought, the body was in the water already, so she doubted any evidence would be in pristine condition. She reminded herself that she didn't even know if a crime had been committed.

Officer Freddy interrupted Dana's internal conversation.

"I need to ask you some questions."

"Um, sure," Dana said, not thinking she could be of any help.

He asked her the usual stuff they asked on those TV shows: what were you doing out here? How did you spot the body from where you were? Did you recognize the body?

She answered his questions. "I was on a run. I stopped to rest and take in the amazing views when I saw something floating from the corner of my eye. I didn't look too close, but she was floating facedown, so I don't who it is, but I noticed she was a blonde."

"How do you know she was a she?"

"The long blonde hair and the silk pink pajamas," Dana replied. She was surprised she had spouted that off, not having realized her brain had kept that information.

In her head, she glanced over for a second, saw a dead body, and went posthaste back to town. But she must have gotten a better look than she wanted to admit.

Officer Freddy jotted down notes with a black BIC pen on a pocket notebook, then turned to ask Benny a few questions about how he fit into everything. He answered his questions.

It was all friendly enough. The area was small enough that you got to know everyone that lived nearby on a full-time basis.

Officer Freddy was the cop that was usually sent to Mariposa Beach when the police was needed to deal with the small stuff: a pickpocketed tourist, thieves that stole a swimmer's bag from the beach while they were in the water, a rental car that was broken into, or two drunks getting into a shoving match at the bar.

Dana had gotten to know Officer Freddy pretty well since

she moved to town. She thought he was a good cop. Honest. Diligent. Fair. A nice guy.

He was thirty, but he looked like a scrawny teenager.

"Can you tell me what happened to her?" Dana asked.

Officer Freddy seemed to mull the question over in his head like he was debating how much to share with them.

"Well, that will be up to the detectives and the medical examiner to figure out for sure, but from what I can tell, I would think her death was not an accident."

Officer Freddy's words shocked Dana. She looked at Benny, and his face was also in dismay.

"What makes you believe that?" Benny asked.

"She's floating facedown in the water. I saw severe trauma to the back of the head. But it's way too early, she could have just fallen and hit the back of head."

The rain began to come down, but it was still light. Like a mist.

"It will take the detectives over an hour to get here from Nicoya, and the rain is going to get worse. Can I take Dana back to her house?" Benny asked.

Officer Freddy mulled it over again. It seemed he always thought before speaking, which was actually a smart habit to have, Dana thought.

"Sure. No need to stand out here in the rain waiting for their arrival. I know where to find you."

Officer Freddy was being nice, but the way he said that gave her goose bumps. *I know where to find you.*

Since arriving in town, Dana's interaction with the OIJ detectives so far hadn't been as pleasant as it had been with Officer Freddy of the Tourist Police.

This was true especially with the lead detective, Jorge Picado. She hoped he wouldn't be the one coming to town.

They must have other detectives they could send down, she hoped.

Dana thanked Freddy, and she climbed into Benny's white Land Cruiser and they drove away.

Dana turned back, and she saw Officer Freddy heading back to the rocks.

She was intrigued with what he had said about not thinking the person's death was an accident. Then she started to replay what she had seen back in her head. This time it was if she was hitting the slow-motion button in her brain so she could get a closer look at what she had seen.

She shuddered at what she was seeing. The body seemed to be that of a young person, and she was seeing nails painted in a bright orange color.

The rain began to come down hard, snapping her out of those dark thoughts.

She shivered.

"Are you holding up?" Benny asked.

"Glad we're not out there standing under this downpour with Freddy," she replied.

Benny nodded in agreement.

Dana imagined Freddy standing out there by the rocks in the heavy rain. He would be out in that rain for a while, and he didn't have the shelter of a car, just his motorcycle. *Poor Freddy,* Dana thought.

Another thought crept into her head. She was sure they would send Detective Jorge Picado to investigate.

He was surly and bad-tempered, and he would hit the roof when he found out she was mixed up in yet another murder in Mariposa Beach.

NINE

"How you doing?" Benny asked Dana as he drove from the beach towards Casa Verde.

"Feeling freaked out," Dana replied nervously.

"Anyone would feel that way after finding a body," Benny said. He was trying to sound calm and reassuring for her, but she knew he too was freaking out. She was getting to know him better, and she could see it in his eyes and his body demeanor when he worried.

She also felt guilty that she didn't want Detective Picado to be assigned to the investigation. His reputation as a top-notch detective was undisputed, but so was his reputation for having all the charm of a honey badger, a porcupine, and a skunk rolled into one, but surely she could put up with him to ensure the victim gets the justice she deserved.

It was hard for her not to feel that dread, though. She always seemed to be at loggerheads with Picado, and the thought of seeing him again made her feel queasy.

"I'm thinking the odds are slim that Detective Picado isn't on his way down to investigate as we speak," she said, sounding nervous.

"Unless he's been reassigned or transferred elsewhere, I think you're correct."

Dana sighed loudly.

"Hey, forget him, you've done nothing wrong. All you need to do is tell him how you found the body and that's it with your involvement. He gets nasty and I can step in."

Dana smiled. "As my lawyer?" she asked sheepishly.

"Well, yes, because if I step in as your boyfriend, I might be under arrest for punching a detective." He had a goofy grin on his face that made him look so cute, but she knew that Benny really wasn't one to let his fists do the talking.

"Been in a lot of fights, have you?" she said teasingly.

"Not really. Come to think about it, my last physical fight was in fifth grade."

"What was her name?" Dana was grinning widely.

"Rosa Maria. But she was big and tough. About a foot taller than me. I swear," Benny said as they both broke out laughing.

Dana took pride in being a strong-willed, independent woman. She had worked as a journalist for the largest newspaper in San Francisco. Then she worked in public relations, where she had worked for some scuzzy clients and where fending off inappropriate male behavior was a necessary skill to have as a professional woman.

She had moved down to a new country on her own and started her own business. So she liked not having to rely on anyone but herself. It was a trait she had picked up after a bad marriage, nasty divorce, and even from her childhood, where she had a well-meaning but overbearing and judgmental mother. So she had learned to do things her way and didn't like to count on anyone. She knew that wasn't a positive trait to have, and she had been working on herself the last few years because no woman can be an island to herself.

In the past, she would have balked at Benny helping her out

as much as he had since she came to town, but now she welcomed his help. And when he became protective of her, talking tough about punching a police detective on her behalf—even though she knew he would never do that and she didn't want him to do that—she had to admit that she liked it when Benny tried to be her knight in shining armor and found it adorable.

Without his legal expertize to navigate the complicated Costa Rican real estate laws when she inherited Casa Verde, the volumes paperwork involved with legal residency and the even more complicated legal matters that came with opening a business as an expat, she would have been lost without him.

She had been attracted to Benny from the start. He was handsome, with his wavy brown hair and olive skin, so it wasn't too shocking to fathom that she developed a crush on her lawyer pretty quickly.

They had great chemistry from the start, but they kept their relationship professional, much to the chagrin of Dana's best friend, Courtney Lowe. And she didn't even want to think about her mom, who never liked her former husband and then had made it her mission to find her a new one that she would approve of, a thought that made Dana shiver whenever it popped into her head.

Her seventy-nine-year-old mom lived in Petaluma, a small town in Sonoma County in California's Wine Country, about forty miles north of San Francisco. She felt hurt that her mom hadn't come down to visit her; she even offered to pay for her ticket. But their relationship had never been a close one. She had been close to her dad, who died ten years ago.

Her friend Courtney lived in Dana's hometown of San Francisco, but she had come down to Mariposa Beach when Dana first moved down to help her with the transition and had come down when she had opened her store, so she knew Benny well and wanted nothing more than for those two to take their relationship to the next level. She had been ecstatic when a few months ago they did just that.

They arrived at Casa Verde a few minutes later, and Benny opened the large green front gate with the remote control device Dana had given him to keep in his SUV. He drove up the long, gravel driveway from the front gate to her house, which was flanked by a beautifully tended garden on both sides.

The garden was lush and green from all the rain. Colorful tropical flowers were soaking in the rain. The garden flanked the driveway on both sides, along with flowering trees of mango, avocado, yuca, and banana.

At the front of the house, protected from the rains, were large concrete flower planters with beautiful roses and orchids. Her caretaker, Ramón, had the greenest thumb she had ever seen. She couldn't keep a cactus alive, and Ramón had those beautiful roses and orchids looking beautiful year-round.

Ramón, the man responsible for the beautiful garden, and his wife Carmen stood under a large golf umbrella on the side of the driveway, looking worried.

"We were so worried. You went for your run and you were gone a long time, and when we saw Don Benny's car, we thought, Madre de Dios, something happened to Doña Dana," Carmen said in Spanish as Ramón nodded in agreement.

Dana's uncle had hired them, and when he died and left the property to Dana, she had to decide on what to do about Ramón and Carmen.

For someone from the United States, it seemed like an odd arrangement. She had never had a live-in gardener. And although she had a house-cleaning service that came in once a month, the thought of a housekeeper living on the property was just as strange and made her feel awkward.

It was Benny that had explained to her that these types of arrangements were common in Costa Rica, especially for a large property like Casa Verde.

Her uncle cared deeply for Ramón and Carmen, and he made it clear in his will that they should be allowed to remain on the property after his death.

Dana honored her uncle's wishes. Benny had also vouched for the couple as being hardworking and honest, and it would be great to have them keep an eye on the home, since word would get out that she lived alone, making it a too tempting of a target for burglars to pass up.

She quickly became used to the arrangement and had grown to really care for Ramón and Carmen. She liked that they lived nearby on the property, so she didn't have to worry about going out of town and leaving her house empty.

Ramón's talents exceeded his amazing green thumb gardening skills. He was also a fantastic handyman who repaired the little things that usually went wrong in a house. And if the job was above his skill level—like the time she needed an electrician—he knew whom to call and he ensured she was charged the local tico rate, not the gringo rate.

She would be lost without them, and she was so glad they were in her life.

"I'm so sorry, Ramón, I should have called. I had an unbelievable morning."

Dana filled Ramón and Carmen in with what happened.

"Madre de Dios," Carmen said again, doing the sign of the cross.

Dana asked Ramón to keep his eyes peeled for the arrival of the OIJ within the next few hours.

"The OIJ?" Ramón said, sounding worried all over again.

"Well, Officer Freddy seems to think there might have been foul play involved in the death of that poor woman. He's just guessing. A feeling he has from what he could see of the body. We won't be sure until the medical examiner makes the cause of death official, and they're also on the way down from San José."

"Okay, I'll keep my eyes peeled."

Dana thanked Ramón and Carmen, and she and Benny went inside to the house. They toweled off from the rain and then went to the kitchen. The nervousness of what was going on made her parched so she drank what she felt was about a gallon of water. Then she poured herself and Benny mango juice made from scratch by Carmen from fruits picked right from her own mango trees. She still got a kick out of that every time she took a sip. She would look out her window and could see where those mangos came from. Talk about farm to table, she would giggle. In San Francisco, you could order farmer boxes delivered to your home for a princely sum. It cost an arm and a leg to eat and drink healthy in San Francisco.

"Coffee?" he asked.

"I'd love some, but what I would love even more right now is a nice hot bath," Dana said. She was soaked in sweat from her mad dash and from the rain. And although she wasn't about to share this with Benny, she had sand everywhere... everywhere.

Benny smiled. "Okay. You go take your bath. Relax a bit. I'll go out to Mindy's to pick up some coffee and bagels for us."

"That would be amazing. Oh, shoot, Mindy. Can you let her know what's going on and let her know I'll be in as soon as I can?" Dana hated not showing up to help at the bookstore slash coffee shop, but she knew Mindy would understand. Finding a dead body tended to create havoc on a person's regular day.

TEN

Benny returned almost thirty minutes later with the coffee and bagels.

After taking a smoothing warm bath, Dana slipped on her plush terry-cotton bathrobe and slippers. She brushed her wet hair then went outside to hang out in her favorite spot of the house, the second-floor wraparound veranda, which overlooked the Pacific Ocean off in the distance and the lush green foliage of the forest off to the side. The veranda was only accessible from her master bedroom, and it was where she spent a lot of her free time.

The rain had let off a bit but it was still coming down steadily but she stayed dry under the the roof that covered the veranda.

"Sorry, it took me longer than I expected," Benny said as he walked out to the veranda. "Word is out that you found a dead body, and the town is buzzing with the news. I guess a crowd has already gathered around the spot where you found the body, so Officer Freddy has his hands full trying to keep the gawkers away from the crime scene."

"Oh, that's dreadful. Bunch of ghouls," Dana said.

Benny nodded in agreement.

"I would give anything to unsee the dead body of that poor woman, and there are people heading out to the rocks, hoping to catch a glimpse of the body."

She felt her body trembling again.

Dana was curled up on a chaise lounge chair with Wally, who had curled up next to her. Benny sat down on the chair next to her. Wally turned his head, giving him a side-eyed glare as if warning him he wasn't moving.

"Sorry, no room for you," Dana said, smiling.

"I don't think your cat likes me much."

"Oh, Wally is just a little jealous, that's all." Dana scratched the top of his head and his chin, causing him to melt like butter in her hand. His eyes were tightly shut, and he was purring loudly.

"See, he's so sweet," Dana cooed.

"Yeah, with you. I've seen his claws. I'm not messing with him." Benny laughed.

He placed the coffee cups and the bagels on the table.

"Mindy made pineapple empanadas, my weakness, so I bought a few of them for later."

"Mmm, smells wonderful, thank you."

Wally perked up at the sight and smell of the goodies. He got up, stretched, and meandered over towards the food.

"Don't you dare, mister," Dana said to Wally, who gave her *a what, me* look. "Yeah, you."

It wasn't working, so he shook her off and tried his luck with Benny.

"Oh, now he's my friend," Benny said, smiling. He tore off a chunk of bagel and fed it to the eager cat.

"Benny, you're spoiling him."

"Hey, I need to curry all the favor I can with him. And who knew cats liked bagels?"

They both laughed, and they ate their food and drank the rich dark coffee.

"Did you go out to the rocks?" Dana asked nonchalantly.

"No way. I don't want to go back there knowing there's still a body there. I just talked to Mindy and a couple of the regulars who were heading out there to go snoop."

"I wonder how long before the detectives get to town. I'm not too keen to sitting around all day waiting for them."

"No need. Carry on with your regular routine. Mariposa Beach is small enough that they'll find you easily if they need to."

"That's true. Besides, if I'm not home, odds are good that I'm at the store. I'm way too predictable."

Benny had planned to head back to San José the following morning, but with the hubbub enveloping Mariposa Beach and Dana herself in the thick of things, he decided to stick around for a few days, so he told her that.

"You don't have to do that," Dana said.

"I don't have to... but I want to."

"What about work?"

"A nice perk of having my solo law practice is that I'm the boss, and I'm a pretty flexible boss, if I don't mind saying so myself. Besides, I don't have any closings until next week, so I can work from down here. Thank you, Wi-Fi and mobile phones. If I leave, I would go crazy wondering what's happening, so I'll be more focused working from here for the next few days, anyway."

Dana thanked him. She couldn't hide the fact that she was happy that Benny was sticking around longer, especially since she was sure that Detective Picado was heading to town.

She shuddered to think about having to be face-to-face with that surly man again.

She had first met the homicide detective her first week in

town. She had just moved into Casa Verde, and her cousin, who had been contesting her uncle's will which left the house and property to her and not his estranged son, was murdered.

Since they were involved in a legal dispute over a lucrative property, she became a prime suspect, and Detective Picado zeroed in on her, making her life quite terrible until finally the real killer was discovered.

Picado wasn't too happy that she had been the one to find out who had murdered her cousin, not the detective, and that he had focused his attention on the wrong person: Dana.

Even after he had warned her many times to butt out of his investigation, she wasn't going to sit around as he built a case around her because he had blinders on when it came to finding the killer. Once that had all been resolved and she got a lot of the credit, he had become even meaner towards her.

Luckily, he was stationed and lived in Nicoya, which was about an hour away, so she only had to deal with him when something happened in town that required the OIJ to investigate.

Unluckily for her, she seemed to be in the thick of things the last time he was in town investigating a murder that had taken place in her bookstore, and now there was another body. And she found it. Picado would be on her like white on rice. She just knew it.

ELEVEN

Dana and Benny enjoyed the bagels and the coffee. They also split one of Mindy's pineapple empanadas that were becoming quite famous up and down the coast, even though they were meant for a later snack.

She decided to stay at home not wanting to face the towns-folk asking her questions at the bookstore slash cafe.

After a couple hours, Benny left to pick up his laptop at his house. He had left in such a rush when Dana had called about the dead body that he had run out of the house with just his wallet and his phone.

Dana was up on her veranda, reading a Sue Grafton novel on her Kindle, but she couldn't really focus on it. Her mind kept drifting back to the morning and finding that body floating in the shallow water. Her phone rang, making her jump. She picked it up, and it was Amalfi Soto calling from the bookstore, so she took the call.

Amalfi sounded flustered over the phone.

"What is it, Amalfi?"

"The OIJ detectives was just here looking for you," she said, getting even more agitated.

"It's okay, Amalfi. They just need to talk to me about the body I found this morning."

"Well, he was nasty and was very upset you weren't here."

"Let me guess, his last name is Picado?"

"That's him. He terrified me. Reminded me of my manager at the resort."

Like most of the local youth that lived in the beach and mountain towns around the peninsula, she had worked at the Tranquil Bay Resort. She didn't like the atmosphere of working there, since the owner, Gustavo Barca, believed in the heavy-handed management style. Since the fish rots from the head down, the managers and supervisors followed suit by kissing up and kicking down by bullying the staff. Amalfi hated working there, but she needed the job. Dana was looking for someone to work at the bookstore, so when she had heard about Amalfi's poor treatment at the resort, she offered her a job that Amalfi happily accepted.

"Oh, he's just a big bully. If he needs to talk to me that bad, he knows where I live."

"He said that's just where he was going next."

"Now?"

"That's what he said."

"How long ago?"

"He just left."

Crap, Dana thought. "Okay, thanks for the heads-up. I'll be there as soon as I can. Don't engage anyone sniffing around for gossip. Especially the ladies from the Gossip Brigade. Just say you know nothing."

"Well, I don't really know much," Amalfi replied.

"That makes two of us. See you in a bit," Dana said, hanging up the phone.

Oh, that jerk, Dana thought as she sent Benny a text, letting him know Picado was on his way.

He texted back right away: On my way!

The bookstore slash cafe was a five-minute drive away from Dana's house. Benny's beach house was on the outskirts of town, about a ten-minute drive away in the gravely, pot-holed, one-lane road that cut across town towards the turnoff to a dirt road that made its way up towards the mountains and to Dana's home, Casa Verde.

Dana wasn't looking forward to dealing with Picado without Benny, but there was no way she would let the detective see that he made her nervous, so she began to psych herself up like a boxer before a big fight. At least that's what she had seen the boxers do in the movies.

Dana had been lost in thought for a couple minutes when suddenly the front gate trilled, snapping her back to reality.

After having dealt with a homicidal nutjob when she first moved to town, Dana invested in a state-of-the-art security system for Casa Verde.

The front gate intercom had an HD video camera, so she looked at the app on her laptop that showed the entire camera feeds from her security system. She saw a white sedan parked there and Detective Gabriela Rojas in the driver's seat. She was leaning out the driver's-side window, looking into the camera and smiling.

That meant, that as usual, Picado was in the passenger's side. He always made the junior detective drive. It surprised Dana he didn't insist on riding in the back like she was his chauffeur.

Detective Rojas was actually nice. Dana got along well with her. She wasn't sure if it was a good cop, bad cop thing going between those two; she doubted it, but if they did that on purpose, they were doing a heck of a job at it, because as far as she was concerned, when it came to temperament and personality, Rojas was the good cop and Picado the bad cop.

Dana pressed the intercom button and told them to come on up. She then pressed the button to open the front gate to let the detective drive onto her property.

They drove the same car they had been tooling around town the last time she saw them. It was an unmarked white Toyota Yaris hatchback. The drive from the front gate to her front door took about a minute on a long and winding gravel road though her property.

The house sat on top of the hill. It had been built that way to take advantage of the breathtaking views of the Pacific Ocean to the south and the lush greenery of the forest to the north. The views were especially spectacular from Dana's favorite spot in the upstairs veranda, where she could scan the entire property from up in her perch, which Benny jokingly called her sniper's nest.

Dana was standing there watching as she heard the tires crunching gravel as the car made its way up to the house.

She sighed heavily and made her way downstairs to greet her unwanted visitors.

TWELVE

Detective Picado didn't pack an imposing physique—far from it. At five feet six inches tall, he wasn't much taller than her, so she could have conversations with him eye to eye.

He was slim and lean, with little muscular definition from what she could tell, since he seemed to always wear the same gray suit.

He reminded Dana of one of those featherweight boxers. He had a bushy black Tom Selleck-like mustache. He kept his black hair short and combed to the side. He wore a suit even during the thick of the summer months, when wearing a suit and tie made it seem like a sadist choice, yet Dana never saw him sweat. Not even a bead. She thought he must be an alien or something, or he must change suits several times throughout the day.

But despite the less than impressive physical attributes, he gave off an aura that was intimidating to behold.

He also had an uncanny ability to go a long time without blinking, as if he was drilling into your eyes and boring into your soul. Dana figured it was a learned trait he used to spook suspects and witnesses during interviews and interrogations. It was weird and freaky, and Dana figured it must work darn well, because it unnerved her.

Like he was a robot rebooting.

Dana opened the door as the two detectives climbed out of the car.

"Hi, Dana," Gabriela Rojas said in her usual friendly voice. Picado said nothing as the pair of detectives made their way up the front steps, where Dana stood waiting for them in the foyer.

"Please come in." Dana managed a smile.

Detective Gabriela Rojas was the polar opposite of Picado. She was always friendly, with a quick smile, and she oozed empathy.

It was an odd pairing, but Dana figured the top brass knew it was best to pair the ornery and rude Picado with a partner that possessed the people skills he so sorely lacked. Dana assumed a big part of her job was smoothing over any feathers Picado would ruffle up during an investigation. The man had no filter. And to his credit, she had seen him treat everyone, regardless of class, economic standing, sex, or race in the same awful, curt, rude way.

"Ms. Kirkpatrick," Picado hissed as they made their way inside.

Dana gave him a quick nod. It's about all he deserved from her as far as she was concerned.

She invited them to sit in the living room. She offered something to drink, but both detectives declined.

"Well," Picado said, sitting down on an armchair, "it appears whenever there is a dead body in Mariposa Azul Beach, you're involved in it."

Ding, ding, ding, there he goes. In less than a minute.

He was also the only person who always referred to Mariposa Beach by its full official name of Mariposa Azul Beach —

named after the famed blue morpho butterfly found in Costa Rica.

Dana frowned. "Gee, you really know how to butter up a witness."

Picado shrugged. "The only thing I ever butter up is my bread."

Lame burn. Dana's eyes rolled. Off to a great start.

"Well, it's a horrifying experience that's hard to shake. But I'm doing okay, psychologically. Not that you asked or care about that."

"I'm glad you're doing okay. I can imagine how traumatic it has been for you," Rojas said.

Picado didn't acknowledge the topic. He cleared his throat. "Now," he said, removing a notebook and pen from an inside coat pocket, "I'd like to ask you some questions about the latest body you've found." His voice sounded even more contentious towards her than usual.

He's on a roll, Dana thought. She let his bad attitude slide right off her. She sat down on the sofa across the chairs that Picado and Gabriela sat on. Dana crossed her legs and said, "Okay, ask away."

He flipped through a few pages in his notebook and he jotted into it with a fancy-looking silver pen. Dana glanced down, and he was writing down the date and her name. *"Testigo"* was written in parentheses next to her name. That was the Spanish word for *witness*. *Thank goodness*, Dana thought, *he's treating me like a witness and not a suspect for a change.*

Once he was done jotting on the page in his notebook, he looked up at Dana and said, "All right, start from the beginning. Don't leave out any details. Even if you think something isn't important, I want to know about it. I'll make the determination if something is of importance or not."

"From when I found the body?"

"No. I want to know about every single step you took that morning that led to you discovering the body. What time you woke up, if you saw a crab crawling near the crime scene. Any detail, I want to know about it."

No pressure Dana, she thought as she sighed loudly.

For the next few minutes, Dana did just that. She told them about getting up and going for a morning run from her house down to the beach. How she would then run on the beach up to the rocks before turning back and running back home.

How she had stopped by the rocks to catch her breath and enjoy the ocean views when something caught her eye peripherally.

How she thought it was garbage, debris that's commonly found on the coast. How she picked up a piece of driftwood so she could remove the garbage from the water so it wouldn't get washed out back into the ocean. How she got close enough to determine she was looking at a dead body that had washed up on the rocks from somewhere out in the water.

"How do you know that the body drifted in from the ocean and washed up on those rocks?" Picado asked.

"I don't. I just assume."

"Don't."

"What?"

"Don't assume. Just give me the facts."

Did he just go Joe Friday on me?

She couldn't help but smile. It was like she was in an episode of *Dragnet*.

"Okay..." Dana described with just the facts how the body was facedown in the shallow water between two large boulders. And how the body swayed gently with each incoming wave. Strands of long blonde hair and silk pink pajamas swayed gently in the water as if it were a blanket.

"Did you touch the body?"

"Oh, heck no. Gross."

"You didn't check to see if the person was alive?"

"I stood over the body for a few seconds. It was facedown in the water. Unless she was the Queen of Atlantis, that person was dead. I wasn't about to go poking at a dead body to confirm the obvious."

Dana saw Gabriela bite her lip, trying to prevent a smile from creeping up.

"So what did you do next?" Picado asked.

"I got the heck out of there. Ran as fast as I could back to the Qué Vista Restaurant because I had seen Julio with a truck delivery guy when I ran past the restaurant on my way to the beach. I asked Julio to call the police, and he did. Then Freddy got down here on his motorcycle pretty quickly."

"And you waited for Officer Freddy at the restaurant?"

Dana knew Picado already knew these details from Officer Freddy's own account and reports, but she was aware part of the detective's job was to go over every little detail in ad nauseam even if he had heard the same thing from fifty different people already. It was to see if they could pick up nuances that might lead to better information or to outright lies or mistakes on the timing of things. Dana had nothing to hide, so she continued answering his questions. She was feeling relaxed.

"Yes, I waited for the police at the restaurant."

They were ten minutes into the interview when Benny arrived. He had a remote control to the front gate, so he drove on up and walked inside without knocking or ringing the bell.

"Good morning, detectives," he said, walking towards the gathering in the living room.

Picado glared at him, annoyed at the interruption.

Benny sat next to Dana on the couch. "How are you doing?" he asked her quietly.

"She's fine. Can we continue with the interview you interrupted?" Picado said before Dana could answer him.

Dana smiled at Picado's rudeness, and she turned to Benny and said, "I'm fine. The detective is just asking questions about this morning and I'm answering them." She then turned to Picado and said, "Aren't I, Detective?"

He grunted, and she smiled. It was petty, but it felt good making him even more annoyed than he usually was in his normal state.

The interview lasted for another thirty minutes, which to Dana seemed about twenty-eight minutes more than necessary. She went on a run. Found a body. Called the police. That's all she knew. But he kept asking questions.

"Did you know the victim?"

"She was facedown in shallow water. I didn't see her face. She was blonde. Most blondes around here are tourists, so I'm assuming she was a tourist."

"Have you identified her?" Benny asked.

Picado mulled over the question. Gabriela looked over at him and he gave her a quick go-ahead nod, so she answered Benny's question.

"She was an American. She was here for that reality television show that's being filmed on Isla Santa Rita. Her name was Rose Budd. Do you know her by name?"

Picado was quiet. He was watching Dana intently so he could gauge her reaction.

Dana put her hand over her mouth. Benny sat back in disbelief.

"Holy crap! That's her, Benny," she said, digging her nails into Benny's arm.

"So you knew the victim?" Picado asked, eyes wide.

"Well, no, we just met her one time, briefly."

"When?"

"A few days ago. We were waiting for a table at Qué Vista and she was there with a boyfriend and they got into an awful and loud fight, in front of everyone. It was quite the scene, with glassware being thrown at people and to the floor."

"How do you know that person was Rose Budd?"

Dana explained how Rose's date had told her who she was before he stormed off, leaving her alone. And how she was so drunk and belligerent that Benny, Maria Rivera—the restaurant's owner—and Julio, her head waiter had taken her outside because Maria wanted her out of her restaurant over her unacceptable drunken and belligerent behavior.

Then Dana told them about Russ Donnelly, the creator and executive producer of the show who showed up in a black Range Rover. He also told them she was Rose Budd. And how he had whisked her away, tossing a few hundred dollars to Maria for her inconvenience and damages.

Picado and Rojas took notes continuously. Picado was scribbling notes into his little notebook while Rojas—who was about twenty years younger than Picado—tapped notes into her mobile phone.

"And that's the last you saw of her?" Picado asked.

"Yes. That was the one and only time," Dana replied.

"According to Russ Donnelly, they were all heading out to the island for the show and they wouldn't be around town for a while," Benny added.

"The next day, I saw the whole crew down at the pier; they were boarding equipment into two boats as they prepared to leave. It got nice and quiet after they all left."

"Did you see Ms. Budd on a boat?" Rojas asked.

"No. There were a bunch of people, but I guess they were all crew. The cast must have been taken to the island on a separate boat."

"How do you know this?"

"I don't know, I'm just assumi... guessing."

"Stop guessing and assuming," Picado snorted.

"You told me to tell you anything, so that's what I'm doing, sharing stuff just in case it might matter."

Picado shot her a look but said nothing, since she was doing just what he asked. She savored the moment.

"Guessing and speculation is not helpful," Picado said, scribbling into his notebook.

She was getting ready to give him a piece of her mind, but Benny must have sensed that coming, so he gently put his hand on her arm as if to say *let it go, he's not worth it.*

So Dana regained her composure and ignored the snide remarks.

"So you never saw Ms. Rose Budd or her boyfriend, Robbie Gibbons, since that night?"

"No. I hadn't really even thought about either of them until now that you said she's the one I found. It makes this even creepier," Dana said, rubbing the hairs on her arm that had stood up from the chills triggered by the knowledge that the body she found was Rose Budd.

"Have you determined if she died accidentally?" Benny asked.

Picado once again appeared to be thinking about how much information he would share with them.

"The body was taken to San José by the medical examiner this afternoon. We don't have an official ruling yet, but from my vast experience as a homicide investigator and from talking to the forensic specialists that processed the body at the crime scene, I believe the death was not accidental; Ms. Rose Budd was murdered."

The hairs on Dana's arms now stood at full attention, and she felt a tremble from head to toe.

THIRTEEN

Dana loved being part of the Calbears Swimming and Diving team at the University of California, Berkeley.

She stood at the top of a very high diving board. It was the longest distance to the pool that she had even seen, well beyond the collegiate standards she had been used to. The distance frightened her.

She wore a one-piece Berkeley blue swimsuit with the logo for the California Golden Bears emblazoned on the suit right in the middle of her chest. A California gold-colored swim cap covered her head.

She looked down below. She felt her hands getting sweaty. She looked down below one more time and shook her head. It seemed dangerous and unreal, but she went for it. No fear. She bounced on the edge of the board and dived into the pool down below. She seemed to be in the air for hours until finally she hit the water.

She executed a beautifully clean dive into the pool. She knew it was a good dive as she swam up to the surface, eager to see the judges' scores.

She popped her head out of the water with a wide smile but

then was surprised that she was all alone in a very large pool. After a moment of confusion, she tried to get out of the pool. She looked around, trying to figure out how to get out, but she couldn't find one. There weren't any ladders or a way out, and the edge of the pool seemed miles and miles away.

She became even more confused. She panicked when she saw a blond-haired body, facedown in the water, wearing pink silk pajamas, slowly floating towards her. She noticed the bright orange nail polish. She again tried to get out of the pool, but realized she was inside a large, silo-like structure with flat walls, impossible to climb. She looked up, but above her was pitch-darkness. She felt her body going into full panic mode, hyper-ventilating, swallowing water until she coughed and gagged.

She was desperately trying to figure out how to get out the water—there wasn't a way out. She looked back towards the body, blonde hair floating around it like a bright yellow aura.

It was slowly floating in closer and closer to where she was wading in the water helplessly. Suddenly, she heard a loud, guttural grunting sound. It was terrifying, and it was becoming louder and louder as the body floated closer and closer to her.

Dana tried to figure out what she was hearing and who was making that sound. Was it a scream? No, it was a howl? It was animalistic. Wait, was that... Napoleon? The howler money that lived out in the woods on the other side of the wall of her property. It was Napoleon, and boom—she awakened from a horrible nightmare.

She sat up on her bed, straight and stiff like an ironing board.

Her heart was beating so fast, it hurt. She was sweating. She could feel her T-shirt damp from it. And she felt nervous and scared, but slowly those feelings began to dissipate as she realized it was just a nightmare and she was awake safe and sound in her own bed with Wally looking at her like she had lost her mind.

That was when she heard the howler monkey barking at the moon again, and she smiled. It was the howler money they named Napoleon because he was short but feisty, which reminded Dana and Courtney of the French despot.

Thank goodness. She had never been so happy to hear those monkey sounds that had jarred her awake from that awful nightmare.

There were several types of monkeys living in the Costa Rican woods. The howler monkey was the most abundant around Mariposa Beach, and also the loudest.

They looked cute as a button, but at night they liked to emit these loud grunting howls that Dana swore could be heard from miles away.

Napoleon lived so close to her property that his howls would jolt a person out of a bed, thinking King Kong was right outside, waiting to snatch them from bed à la Fay Wray.

Dana had become accustomed to the howls. It was like people living by railroad tracks. After a while, they couldn't even tell a train was going by even though it was shaking and rattling the entire house.

Same thing with the howler monkeys, but on that night, during that nightmare, she was grateful that Napoleon's howls had snapped her from her frightening slumber.

She wanted to think Napoleon knew she was having a horrible nightmare, so he howled even louder than usual to wake her up.

"Thanks, Nap," she said out loud as she stood by the window, getting some fresh air. It was pitch-dark outside, but she looked out towards the forest where Napoleon and his fellow monkeys seemed to have quite the heated debate about something. It made her think of her best friend, Courtney, and how much she missed her.

It had been Courtney who had anointed the big howler monkey with the name of Napoleon and who had a love-hate relationship with the loud monkeys.

"They were here first," Dana liked to remind her.

Dana smiled at the memory and went back to bed.

She woke up at six a.m., but she felt exhausted. Between the nightmare, the howling all night, and Wally hogging up half the bed, she had gotten very little sleep.

She figured it would be a rough night. The images of the dead body she had found seemed to have been etched into her brain. It was an image she would probably never get out of her head.

The visit from Detective Picado didn't help matters, either. He left her feeling stressed out and anxious. She hated to admit it, but Picado got to her.

Dana always strived to be a positive person, always trying to find good in people even when it might be tough to do so.

So she tried to see things from Picado's perspective. Sure, he was a surly man, but that was just his nature. A lot of surly types in the world. Despite having the personality of a honey badger, he was a seasoned detective with over twenty years of experience on the job who had probably seen so much of the ugliness that humans could inflict on each other that it was not surprising he wasn't the most empathetic person.

Dana figured you had to somewhat disconnect in order to do his job for so many years. It was not surprising that he did not suffer fools or mince words. And he'd become hardened by his job. Dana assumed he must see and think the worst in people because in that business, he saw so much of it.

But after her third encounter with the detective, and try as hard as she may to look at things from his perspective, she finally had decided she did not like him, and that was that.

Sure, he was good at his job, but he was a jerk. Plain and simple. It was pointless trying to season a steak that had gone bad. You just threw it out. So that's what she did with his snarky comments, his glares, and threats. Dana tossed them out to the ether as soon as he left. Or at least that's what she tried to do.

She felt relieved to find out that Picado had plans to get out to the island to interview the cast and crew of the show, so he wouldn't be around town for a day or two. It would be a nice break from the reality that someone had murdered Rose Budd. Dana's only encounter with the self-described model and social media influencer had been awful, but still the poor woman was so young, just in her early twenties, and now she was dead. It was hard to fathom. Dana also wondered what would happen with the production of the reality television show.

Could the show really go on amidst a murder investigation of one of their cast members?

From her brief encounter with the producer, Russ Donnelly, she didn't doubt that was what he would want to do. The show must go on. After all, a one-day delay in the production schedule would cost him thousands of dollars.

Picado was heading over to the island, and Dana cracked a smile, wondering how those two honey badgers would fare with each other.

FOURTEEN

Dana walked out to her veranda. It was a beautiful morning. The rains seemed to be in check. It was one of those mornings when she regretted starting a business so soon after moving to town.

She would much rather go snorkeling or go on a hike or practice on her surfing that she had been learning from Big Mike, or go off-roading in Big Red, but she was headed out to her store.

Well, no duh, dummy, she told herself, *who wouldn't want to do those things instead of working?*

She liked to work and keep busy. She knew how blessed she was to be living in a tropical paradise in a beautiful home, that she inherited debt-free. She had left San Francisco with a nice nest egg after the divorce.

California was a community property state, which meant the law presumed all property acquired during the marriage was owned equally by both spouses, so the marital property was divided equally. *Yay for California*, Dana had thought many times during her divorce.

Not like she didn't deserve it. She had been there from the

start when he was just another dorm-living programmer at Stanford and she was the breadwinner when he worked eighteen-hour days for peanuts and the dream that his stock options would amount to something. It was like being married to a poker player.

For every Facebook and Google, there is Myspace and AltaVista. And even more start-ups that never even made it out of the starting gate.

Besides, she could have taken her cheating ex to the cleaners when determining spousal support, but she just wanted him out of her life.

All she wanted from him was her fair share and then to be rid of the philandering lout from her life forever.

So the divorce, although stressful and contentious, had been rather fast and quick.

Dana smiled, remembering how she used that song from the musical *South Pacific*, "I'm Gonna Wash That Man Right Outa My Hair," as her wake-up alarm tone during that ugly time in her life.

She had also been good with her money and had made some wise investments, so although she wasn't rich by any stretch of the imagination, she was more fortunate than most. The cost of living between San Francisco—one of the most expensive cities in the world to live in—and Mariposa Beach would probably break her calculator if she tried to figure out the cost-of-living differences between the two, so she was doing just fine.

But she wasn't about to sit around on the beach at thirty-five. She mulled using her journalism skills to become a travel or Costa Rica expat blogger and vlogger, but she discounted doing that because she really didn't have that self-promotional personality to do well in that younger persons' game of being a YouTuber.

It was interesting. She thought about how that world of

social media and entertainment was dominated by people like Rose Budd and Robbie Gibbons or any of the other castaways filming on the island, who seemed shameless when it came to self-promotion.

A small bookstore and coffee shop were more up her alley.

When she first opened up her bookstore, it had been slow. Most tourists read on their Kindles or on iPads and smart phones. Most travelers nowadays didn't really buy paper books that they must haul around back and forth from home to their vacation destination, especially now that airlines charged a fee for everything. Books added weight to luggage that could tip the scale in having to cough up more money to the airline.

Dana figured soon enough the airlines would install a credit card reader on the door of the tiny bathroom in their airplanes.

Logic also told her that the local market in town wasn't big enough to keep the bookstore in the black, but then her greedy landlord jammed Mindy up, so she moved her cafe into the bookstore. And it had been fantastic.

Books, bagels, and lattes went along like a house on fire. There was a reason you could find a Starbucks inside a Barnes and Noble.

Dana also implemented some new strategies to drum up more business for the books part of the store. She started a lending program, becoming a sort of library where people could rent books and even a fully loaded e-reader for the duration of their trip.

The loaded e-reader became a big hit. People could choose a pre-loaded e-reader based on their favorite genre or author. She had their credit card on file, so if they stole or damaged the e-reader, she could charge them for it.

It had become a popular service, so kept adding more Kindles, Nooks, and Kobo e-readers available for rent. And she had even had requests for a French Bookeen and the German Tolino e-readers.

"You're lucky," she told herself out loud as she thought about how well things were working out for her.

"Are you talking to me, Doña Dana?"

The voice of Ramón, who was down below working on the garden, startled her. He must have heard her talking to herself, giving herself these little morning pep talks. She blushed.

"No, I'm just talking to myself again," she said, looking down from her second-floor deck, feeling embarrassed.

Ramón smiled and waved at her and got on with his work. Dana laughed. *He must think I'm cuckoo.* She went back inside to shower and get ready for the day.

Dana left the house and drove into town. She parked and greeted the parking lot guard, José Luis, who greeted her cheerily. "Good morning, Doña Dana. Are you okay?" he asked her, a worried look on his face.

"I'm fine, José Luis, thank you." She smiled and made her way to her store.

One local waved at her from the street. "Are you doing okay?"

Hmm, word is traveling fast about me finding that dead body, Dana thought as she reassured her too that she was fine.

She finally made it inside at nine o'clock a.m. Amalfi was helping Mindy when the caffeine seekers. Three customers were lined up for their fix, and all three looked at her like she was a zoo animal.

"Good morning, honey, how are you doing?" Mindy asked, sounding worried.

"I got things under control, Doña Dana, if you need some time off," Amalfi said.

Word about me finding the dead body must have reached the Nicaraguan border by now, Dana thought as she smiled.

"No, I'm fine. I need to keep busy."

Amalfi was a real sweetheart, and Dana was so happy Carmen had told her that her niece was looking for a new job. She was a trustworthy and responsible employee, and it was Amalfi who opened the store and manned the register and was happy to help with the cafe.

The only drawback was that Amalfi's English wasn't the best, and most of the customers were tourists or expats from the US and Canada. But Amalfi had been excited about that, since she could practice her English and get better at it. English was a sought-after skill for the locals working in the tourist-dependent province.

She was also determined to make things even better in her life by going to school part time to get her degree in business— the first in her immediate family to do so. She hoped to one day be a business owner like Dana herself.

Dana loved that about her, so she created a college fund for her and encouraged her to follow her dreams and get her education. She also paid for English lessons with a retired ESL teacher from Texas that lived in nearby Samara.

It wasn't like the language barriers had been much of an issue with her customers. Dana was there most days, and Mindy and her husband both spoke English. Besides, only a handful of very rude and entitled customers had the chutzpah to complain about a Costa Rican cashier not being able to speak English very well in a Spanish-speaking country like Costa Rica. But it happened. Entitlement is a vile thing.

Dana settled in. Business was slower now that the production team had moved off to the island, but there was still a large contingent that came back and forth from the island to the mainland.

There also seemed to be a bevy of producer types that were staying in an Airbnb in town, and higher up the producer food chain were a few executives staying at the Tranquil Bay Resort. So there always seemed to be at least a few of the production-team people hanging around the bookstore slash cafe.

Dana wondered how the cast and crew were doing with Detective Picado there. She imagined he arrived on the island as welcomed as a tsunami.

She kept glancing around, hoping one of the crewmembers would stop by so she could ask how the Picado storm front was going.

She was ringing up a customer who rented one of the thriller-loaded e-readers. He was a chatty one. Mike Anderson from Chicago, he had introduced himself.

"Wow, so you're American and you moved here and opened up a business, just like that, huh?"

"Well, sort of... it took cutting through a lot of red tape, and a lot of elbow grease to get things going," Dana said, smiling.

"It's my first time visiting Costa Rica. It's beautiful down here. I can see why you left the rat race to move here." There was a twinge of jealously in his voice.

"It hasn't even been a year yet, but I'm liking the slower pace down here compared to San Francisco."

"So you're from San Fran," the man said, referring to San Francisco in a way that made the locals cringe. Only Frisco was worse. She didn't know when or why San Franciscans took affront over having their city by the bay referred to as San Fran or Frisco, but it had become a thing that even far away in Mariposa Beach she cringed at hearing her home city called by that ghastly name... San Fran.

"You loaded this bad boy with some great stuff. James

Patterson, Walter Mosley, James M. Cain, John Sanford, Peter May, Tess Gerritsen—what a lineup."

Dana smiled. Half the fun was picking which e-books to load on the e-readers.

During the entire conversation, she was waiting for him to ask if she had been the lady who found the dead body, as several strangers and every local that came into the shop had asked her, but to her delight, he didn't. She missed her normal routine before she found the dead body.

FIFTEEN

It was an hour before closing time, and things had really slowed down at the bookstore slash cafe.

Amalfi was doing her homework for her English lesson that evening. Mindy and Leo were trying to get a jump on closing time by cleaning up the kitchen.

There was only one customer in the store. A tourist from the States was drinking a latte and reading a book while his wife was at a yoga class at Marisol Arias's studio, which was three doors away.

Dana was in her back office, working on the receipts of the day. She kept glancing at her computer's monitor. There were six video feeds from her security system.

Benny's friend, Román Garza, who owned a security company in San José, had set up her home security system and done the same for the bookstore so she had access to a nifty video security system where she could monitor what was going on in just about every nook and cranny of her store and outside.

She had learned the hard way that even in a small beach town community, there were a lot of folks with sticky fingers for paperbacks and the other knickknacks she sold.

She didn't want to think it was the locals shoplifting, and preferred to think it was just the tourists or someone passing through to the more popular beaches and to Nosara and Samara.

Dana felt Román had gone a bit overboard with his setup, but he was a former spy, so he was on the paranoid side of things.

She remembered when she first met Román that it surprised her that Costa Rica had a spy agency. Costa Rica had famously disbanded its army after its last Civil War back in the late forties, but the country had its own version of the CIA, the Department of Intelligence and Security, or DIS as they were known, and Garza had worked for them for years before going into private security work.

She soon found that looking at the security video feeds on her monitor could be just as bad of a time suck as Facebook.

She happened to glance at the monitor to see a large crowd of people walking up from the beach area across Main Street and headed towards Ark Row.

"What the heck?" Dana said out loud at seeing the big crowd. They seemed to be heading towards the bookstore slash cafe.

She got up and walked out to the front. Mindy, Leo, and Amalfi were already looking out the front window at the large crowd of people making their way inside.

"Incoming," Leo said as he headed back to the kitchen to brace himself for the orders.

It was bizarre. From one moment to the next, things got hectic with a sudden influx of business that seemed to came out of nowhere as customers began pouring in.

"Did a tour bus pull into town?" Amalfi asked.

Mindy and Dana shrugged their shoulders, not knowing the

answer. Dana had taken off the owner hat and put on her cashier hat.

"You better help Mindy handle the coffee and food orders, and I'll man the register," Dana told Amalfi, who had a relieved look on her face upon getting help to deal with the crowd.

Dana and Mindy couldn't keep up with the coffee and bagel orders, and it seemed no one wanted just a regular old cup of black coffee, instead choosing the single-pour drip, a latte, or a mocha, all which took time to make.

"What is going on?" Dana asked.

"Not sure. Looks like the rush from one of the sightseeing boat tours or one of the big cruise ships, but the timing is way off," Mindy replied as she took the order from another customer that seemed to have jumped out of the pages of *Sports Illustrated*'s swimsuit edition magazine.

That's when it dawned on Dana that all these customers were young men and women. Many of them looked like models.

"Are you here on a model shoot?" Dana finally asked one of the young beauties with shoulder-length brown hair.

She flashed a perfect set of whitened teeth. It was obvious to Dana that she had taken her question as a compliment.

"Well, not like really, like, I have done some modeling, but like not on a full-time basis yet, but that is like my dream job and like my goal. That's why I'm on the show. I'm like hoping it's like my big break," she said wistfully.

Dana hadn't heard so many likes peppered into a conversation since she had lived in LA. But she was intrigued because she thought cast and crew would be on the island shooting for at least a month or longer. They had just left for the island a few days ago.

"Oh, I thought you would be on the island, shooting the show for a while," Dana said.

The castaway frowned and pouted. "Like, that's where

we're supposed to like be, but the police like shut down the production because like there's been an accident, like you see, one of the castaways, like she drowned," she whispered.

"I know what happened to Rose Budd," Dana said.

The vapid castaway looked at Dana wide-eyed, mouth agape, like she had clairvoyant powers.

"I found the body," Dana explained before the young woman's head exploded.

"Oh, I thought you had like supernatural powers or something," she said, half-suppressing a snorting laugh that didn't seem to fit the petite beauty queen.

"Come on, Dakota! Can you stop gabbing to your new BFF so the rest of us can order? I need coffee, now," a shirtless man with what appeared to be twelve-pack abs barked out from the back of the line.

"Yeah, come on, Dakota, hurry up already," the man next in line griped. But unlike the tanned hunk, he had a cherub-looking bearded face and a slight pouch instead of the chiseled abs. He wore a black T-shirt that had the word CREW on it in a large white font.

And there were at least five more people in line behind him.

Dakota gave him an over-the-shoulder half look and snort, as if to say *as if*. She turned back to face Dana. "Hold your horses, TJ," Dakota said dismissively without facing him. She rolled her eyes at Dana and said loud enough for the back of the line to hear, "You have to excuse them. They have no class at all."

Dana felt guilty for starting the gossipy chitchat, so she stepped up to ensure the line was moving again. She didn't get far, since Dakota wasn't done chatting.

"So wow, like you found her. Was she like all gnarly and bent and stuff?" she asked wide-eyed.

Dana took a step back at the crassness.

"Um, well, no, I don't know, I didn't stick around. I ran off and called the police."

"Oh," Dakota said once again, pouting and looking disappointed.

"Rumor has it that she was like messed up pretty bad, so it might like not had been an accident. My luck. I finally catch a big break on a national television show and this happens to me."

"Well, at least that's the only thing that happened to you, unlike poor Rose Budd, who, like, you know, died," Dana said. She tossed in a like in there for good measure, but it didn't look like Dakota picked up on her sarcasm. She just rolled her eyes again and said, "Yeah, I guess."

"Your order will be ready shortly. If you don't mind waiting over there so I can keep the line moving," Dana said, pointing to her left.

"Whatever," Dakota said. She meandered over towards the order pickup area, burying her nose into her smartphone, which was in a pink, faux ruby-encrusted case, as she waited for her skinny caramel macchiato.

"About time," someone yelled out from the back of the line.

Dana was now waiting on the next customer in line, the one Dakota had so dismissively and rudely called TJ.

"Sorry about the delay, sir, we got very busy all at once."

"It's all right. They ordered the entire cast and crew off the island and back to town while the police investigate Rose's death, so we're the first boat to arrive. Two more were right behind, so brace yourself. After a few days on that deserted island, everyone will be mad dashing here for some of that great coffee and those delicious bagels and empanadas that you make," TJ said, looking over at Mindy.

"Thanks, TJ," Mindy said.

Dana didn't recognize him, but he appeared to be a good customer for Mindy to know him by name. His eyes were puffy and red. Dana figured that a lot of the cast and crew would be saddened by what happened to Rose.

TJ placed his order and joined Dakota in the pickup area.

"A fan," Dana said to Mindy teasingly.

"What can I say, he really likes my bagels and pineapple empanadas."

"Wow, so they shut down the filming. That explains the mystery of the sudden business spike," Dana said.

It stayed busy for the next two hours. Dana and Mindy decided to stay open for an extra hour, since it was the slow season anyway. The ka-ching of the register kept going off over and over.

The actual cash register was connected to an iPad, so it was all modern but boring and sterile looking compared to the old grand cashier registers from the past, so Dana had put in an app so it would make that ringing cash register sound every time a sale was recorded. Mindy's husband, Leo, really loved it.

"That sound never gets old," he said, lathering up strawberry cream cheese onto a sesame bagel with a wide grin.

If it were busy like this every day, she would need to hire a few more employees. But Dana, Amalfi, Leo, and Mindy could manage the crowd and orders of the hungry and caffeine-deprived cast and crew of *The Island* well enough.

They probably could have stayed open even longer, but enough was enough. They were running low on coffee and bagels and had run out of all the other goodies, including the popular pineapple empanadas, much to the disappointment of several customers. Finally, during a brief lull of incoming customers, they closed up.

Leo locked the door, flipping the Open sign to Closed, and he had to wave a few people away. Dana, Leo, Mindy, and Amalfi gathered themselves, exhausted. No one said a word, but they all started laughing at the crazy end of the day.

SIXTEEN

Even with the sudden and unexpected surge in business, it didn't take long to tidy up for the day. Mindy and Leo did a good job of keeping the food-preparation area and the coffee machines clean throughout the day so they wouldn't get nailed with a monster cleanup job at closing. Leo was fanatical at cleaning up as you went along, and now Dana could appreciate that zeal because it made going home that much quicker.

Dana and Amalfi cleaned up the front while Leo and Mindy cleaned up the kitchen and back area as Carlos Santana's guitar solo wrapped up the song *Evil Ways* blasting from the store's sound system.

When they were finished, Mindy took off her apron, and she looked outside towards Main Street. Dana, Leo, and Amalfi joined her. They all looked exhausted.

"Looks like Qué Vista and the pulpería will be very busy tonight," Mindy said, looking out as stragglers walked up towards their place only to see the Closed sign, so they turned back, heading in the direction of the pulpería and the restaurant. The pulpería was what ticos called a corner store or a bodega, a small convenience store where people could buy sodas, chips, beer, cigarettes, milk, eggs, and other treats.

Dana agreed, figuring the liquor-serving Qué Vista would get jam-packed with the rambunctious cast and crew of the television show once again.

"The Giggling Dorado is going to be hopping late at night," Leo said.

The town's only watering hole, The Giggling Dorado, was about a mile away from Ark Row on the beach and not within eyesight from the bookstore slash cafe.

"If you don't need me for anything else, Doña Dana, I have to get going. I have my English lesson tonight," Amalfi said with her purse over her shoulder.

"No, thanks for asking. Have a great lesson. It was a crazy day but a great day for business," Dana said as she walked over towards Amalfi and gave her a hug. "You were great. I'll see you tomorrow."

Mindy and Leo were heading out too.

"You're not leaving?" Mindy asked.

"In a bit. I just need to wrap up some administrative stuff I was working on before the surge, then I'm heading home."

"Okay, don't stay too long," Mindy said as she and Leo walked out the door.

Dana locked the door and yawned, then headed back to the office to finish up with the cash receipts. Credit cards were popular, but cash was still king in these rural parts.

She removed the cash, and she split up the bills into Costa Rican colones and US dollars. She shouldn't accept the foreign currency—she chuckled how the US dollars were now foreign currency for her—but sometimes dollars were all a tourist had, and there was only one ATM in town. It was a third-party machine outside of Antonio's pulpería, and each transaction came with hefty international transaction fees on top of whatever the banks overcharged their customers for using an ATM they did not own.

Dana stuffed the cash into two bank deposit envelopes, which she placed into her backpack.

She tapped on her laptop and glanced at the security cameras to make sure no one was loitering out front. It was seven thirty p.m., so it was dark out, and all the other Ark Rows shops had also closed for the day.

Román Garza had set her outdoor video camera with night vision, so she had a good view of the outside from her small back office.

The front camera had a good view of Main Street and of the start of the footpath that led up towards her home and up towards the resort.

She could also see the Qué Vista Restaurant in the distance, so she couldn't see clearly what was going on there too, but she could tell it was getting busier by the minute.

Maria Rivera would have a good night for business. She just hoped she didn't have any more shenanigans from the cast and crew like the other night with Rose Budd and Robbie Gibbons.

That made her think of Rose Budd's body on those rocks, and she shivered. "I'm going home," she said out loud to herself.

She was about to turn off the monitor when she saw a man that looked like the assistant producer, Henry Robertson running down Main Street. He was running fast at a full sprint.

She figured it was odd to go for a night run, since there were potholes the size of lunar craters out there and it got pitch-dark by six o'clock p.m. There was only one street lamp in town, so walking without a flashlight at night could be ankle-twisting treacherous. Running at that clip was playing with fire.

But to each their own, she was thinking when she saw a black Range Rover speeding in front of the camera. It drove by in just a few seconds, but she recognized the car; it looked like

the same one Russ Donnelly had used that day when she met
him at the restaurant when he whisked Rose Budd away.

It was strange, but she didn't make much of it. Main Street
was the only street through town anyway, so if anyone was going
anywhere around town, they had to go down Main Street
regardless if they were in a car, running, walking, biking.

She shrugged it off and powered down the computer and
went home.

Dana got home after eight o'clock. Wally meowed his displea-
sure at her tardy arrival. "Hey, you're the one who doesn't like
hanging out at the bookstore. Some bookstore cat you've turned
out to be," Dana said to the cat.

Benny had been working from home all day, and they
planned to have a late dinner at Qué Vista, but after seeing the
Hollywood invaders overrun the town again, she wasn't too
keen in experiencing dinner with rowdy and probably drunk-as-
skunks cast and crewmembers of the show.

"I'm in the mood for a quiet dinner at home," Dana said over
the phone when Benny called.

"Sounds good to me. I'll see you in about half an hour,"
Benny said.

SEVENTEEN

Benny arrived at Casa Verde at eight thirty p.m., carrying a grocery bag from the Super Fresco Market in town.

"What do you have there?" Dana said as her stomach rumbled from hunger.

"I was able to make it to the market before they closed," he said as he made his way to the kitchen.

Benny plopped the grocery bag on the kitchen's center island and began to remove items. He pulled out one of those readymade, warm-and-waiting-to-be-eaten rotisserie chickens. It smelled delicious, and it worried Dana that Benny would hear her stomach rumbling its loud approval.

Next out of the bag, a container of roasted potatoes, then a caprese salad of fresh tomatoes with mozzarella and basil. And for dessert, two slices of tres leches cake.

"Well done, Benny, that looks amazing," Dana said, eyeing the food.

"I figured it was late, so I wanted to get items ready to chow. I did, however, make that caprese salad at home before I came over," Benny said proudly.

"Everything looks delicious. Thank you for shopping. Now let's eat, I'm starving."

As they ate, they chatted about their day. He was working on a closing he had next week in the city. She told him about how crazy busy the bookstore slash cafe had been from the sudden influx of the cast and crewmembers from the show. They discussed the show getting closed down and the implications that might have for the town and the show.

"I wonder if they will have to delay the season of the show," Dana wondered.

"I would imagine those shows have contingency plans for stuff like this happening, but who knows what will happen."

After dinner, they went upstairs and sat out on the veranda. They were sharing the love seat. There was a nice cool breeze coming off the Pacific, and the rain had miraculously held up that day, which meant Mother Nature would make them pay for the break the next day.

"Nice night for a walk," Dana said. Her head was resting on Benny's chest. Their fingers were locked together lazily.

"It sure is. Looks like the rain will hold off," Benny said, looking up to the sky.

"You want to go on a walk?" Dana asked.

"Sure. Which route?" Benny said.

"I was thinking we walk down towards the Qué Vista Restaurant and then head down to the beach and walk by the water."

"Mmm hmm..." Benny said suspiciously.

"What?"

"You want to snoop around the restaurant to see what's going with that TV show and the case, don't you?"

She smiled. "Maybe." Dana got up. "Aren't you wondering what's going on?"

"We know what's going on. Rose Budd was killed, and

Detective Picado is investigating, and you know he has it in for you, so let's tread lightly in the snooping department."

"Whatever. I'm not messing with his case. We are just going for a walk. We go out on walks all the time. If we pick up some interesting tidbit, so be it. Besides, I doubt Detective Picado will be hanging out there. It's almost ten o'clock at night."

Benny shook his head. "Okay, troublemaker, let's go check it out."

Even though it was late at night, the air still had a tinge of warmth and stickiness to it—this was the tropics, but Dana was getting used it.

People assumed that as a Californian, she was used to the heat. She had to correct them. She was from Northern California. The Bay Area. San Francisco. Where Mark Twain was often misquoted as quipping that "the coldest winter ever spent was a summer in San Francisco."

The fog kept San Francisco cool. It was rarely too hot or cold. It was a big contrast compared to the Guanacaste Province, where the weather was tropical 365/24/7.

It was hot and dry during the summer and hot and wet during the winter.

One of the great perks was that it cut down her wardrobe needs substantially since moving to Mariposa Beach. No heavy coats, sweaters, and the likes. It was thin shirts, shorts, and jeans every day, all year-round.

Dana and Benny strolled down the footpath from Casa Verde to town, hand in hand.

For all the reservations Dana had about getting in a romantic relationship, it was the little things like going on a couple's walk holding hands that she had missed the most.

They made it down to Main Street past Ark Row with all its stores closed.

Only Antonio's pulpería at the very end of Ark Row stayed open late, but even he was closing up shop when Dana and Benny walked by.

"Hi Antonio," Dana said. Antonio, the owner, was outside, rolling his small wooden fruit stand inside for the night.

"Hello. Nice night out."

"It sure is. Did you get some of that extra business from those television people too?"

"I did. It was a good night, but they almost wiped me out clean of my beer supply that's supposed to last me until the next delivery next week. I'm all out of Heineken and Imperial beer already. All I'll have left until Monday is Pilsen beer. I won't hear the end of it from the locals tomorrow."

Dana chuckled. It took some getting used to for her, coming from the land of instant gratification back in the States to a small beach town off the beaten track where merchants were constantly running out of stuff.

No hay, Spanish for "we don't have it," was heard from the merchants in town as often as "should I ring it up for you?"

Dana and Benny said goodnight to Antonio, and they continued on their walk.

It was a short walk from the pulpería to the Qué Vista Restaurant, and from there they were just a few feet from the beach.

Dana was expecting some wild partying going on, but instead it was subdued. Qué Vista was winding down too.

She figured the drinking types had long moved down to the Giggling Dorado. Murray Theriot, an expat from Louisiana, owned the dive bar, and he would stay open as long as he had a crowd willing to spend money or until he ran out of booze. *No hay*.

They made it onto the beach and continued on their walk. It was too dark to see much, but they could hear the waves crashing lazily onto the shore, giving Dana goose bumps. The beauty of the Pacific Ocean never got old for her. Even in the darkness, she took in the beauty of it all.

She looked up to the night sky, and the stars were out in force. It was like nothing she could see living in San Francisco. Too much fog, smog, and city lights to get the light show you could get down in the tropics. You would have to go to the Morrison Planetarium in Golden Gate Park to get a star show like that in San Francisco.

They ran into Maria Rivera, who was walking from the beach back towards her restaurant.

"Hey, Maria, where are you coming from?"

Maria seemed taken aback at running into them.

"Oh, um, I was getting some fresh air before I close the restaurant. It was busy with all the people from the show back in town," she said, sounding frazzled.

"I know what you mean. We got slammed at the cafe at about five. Stayed open an hour longer and still had to turn people away so we could close."

Maria nodded in agreement as she looked behind her, seeming nervous.

"Did you hear anything about the investigation? When will the show resume shooting?" Dana asked her.

"No one has a clue. You know how Detective Picado is. I think he enjoys the power he has in putting people's lives on hold for as long as he wants."

Dana smiled. It seemed there was no love lost between Picado and just about everybody else in town.

"Any more drama like the last time we were at Qué Vista?"

"Nothing that bad, thank goodness."

"Can you believe it? That loudmouth drunk we kicked out

is dead. It's so creepy. And I found the body," Dana said, sending a shiver down her own spine.

"I should have been nicer, I suppose, you never know when someone's number is up in this life," Maria said, trembling.

"She was out-of-hand drunk, shouting, arguing with that boyfriend, breaking your glassware; you have nothing to feel bad about," Benny said.

"How are you doing, finding the body and all?" Maria asked Dana.

"I had a hard time sleeping a couple nights after that. Had some whacky nightmares," Dana replied.

Benny looked at her, surprised, since that was the first time she had shared that with him.

"Have you seen her boyfriend, Robbie Gibbons, around?" Dana asked.

"No. I haven't seen him since that night. But the word around the campfire is that he's devastated over Rose's death," Maria said.

Dana perked up. "Who told you that?"

"No one directly. It's the good old spread of gossip around town. It's on overdrive. And I overheard a couple of the cast members gossiping about it at my restaurant."

"So what did you hear?" Dana asked.

"Well, I overheard one of the tables at the restaurant saying that Robbie took her death hard and then Detective Picado has him shaking in his Givenchy sandals about going to jail."

"That's Picado doing what he does best," Dana said.

"Usually in these kinds of situations the boyfriend is the prime suspect," Benny said.

Dana nodded in agreement, having watched a lot of true crime shows on the Investigation Discovery Channel.

After another few minutes of small talk not related to Rose Budd's death, Dana and Benny continued down onto the beach so that Maria could close her restaurant and so they could finish their late-night stroll.

"Funny running into her out there," Dana said.

"I guess she needed a break," Benny replied.

They had walked hand in hand for just a couple minutes more when she suddenly heard what sounded like someone crying.

It was too dark to see anything, but they looked at each other, puzzled.

"You hear that?" Dana asked.

Benny nodded, then whispered, "I think someone is crying."

"Sobbing," Dana clarified.

They continued walking, heading towards the crying sound.

"Everything okay?" Benny said out to the dark night in the direction of the crying sounds, which immediately stopped as soon as Benny said that.

Then they could hear someone breathing hard through their nose in an attempt to swallow the fact that they had just been crying.

Dana and Benny could see the shape of a person sitting on the soft sand.

"Are you okay?" Dana asked to the shape.

"I'm fine," the shape replied curtly.

Benny used his iPhone flashlight and pointed it towards the direction of the shape, and sitting there on the beach with his legs crossed was the man Dana knew as TJ from earlier that afternoon in her bookstore slash cafe.

It was the chubby, impatient man behind Dakota who, along with Mr. Twelve-Pack Abs, were hurrying Dakota up for chatting with Dana and holding up the line.

He was alone, just sitting there with four empty bottles of Imperial beer in the sand by his feet. There was one unopened bottle by the empties, and he held one bottle that still had beer in it lazily in his right hand.

He must be one of the customers that wiped out Antonio's Imperial beer supply, Dana thought.

"Are you okay, man?" Benny asked, moving closer with his flashlight still shining.

"You mind getting that light out of my face?" TJ asked, sounding upset.

"Oh, yeah, I'm sorry," Benny said, shutting it off. He then repeated the question, "Are you okay?"

"I'm just peachy. I'm in a strange country. I lost my soul mate, and I've just been fired," he said, taking a long drink from the bottle.

"Your soul mate?" Dana asked.

"I came all the way down to this Third World country for this job and now they fire me. A ticket back to LAX is all I get," he said, not answering Dana's question about the soul mate. Instead, he took another huge gulp of beer, emptying the bottle, which he then dropped between his legs on the sand to join the other empty bottles littered in front of him. He immediately picked up the last bottle and, using the bottle opener in his pocketknife, he opened it and flicked the bottle cap onto the sand.

"Maybe you have had enough to drink, buddy," Benny said.

"Forget you! You're not the boss of me. I don't even know you. But I know you," he said, pointing a crooked finger at Dana. As if the score of empty bottles weren't proof enough, he sounded very drunk.

"You were in my bookstore cafe this morning. You ordered a large dark roast coffee and three pineapple empanadas," Dana said.

He lit up. "Oh yeah, I love those empanadas. Do you have any with you?" he asked seriously.

"Um, no, it's the middle of the night and we're just out for a walk."

"Dang it," he said. He took another sip of beer and scrunched his face. Dana figured the beer was getting warm.

"I could use one of those empanadas right about now," he said, sighing loudly.

"So how did you lose your soul mate?" Dana asked.

"The most beautiful girl in the world. She was so talented. A star in the making. Rose Budd... and now... and now... she's dead," he said. He began to sob again. "I loved her so much."

Dana felt a ping inside, for the pain he was feeling felt palpable to her.

"I thought she was with Robbie Gibbons," Benny said, rather coldly.

He might as well have insulted TJ's mother and kicked his puppy, the way TJ glared at Benny.

"She didn't love that idiot pretty boy. She loved me," he said, shoving his thumb onto his chest and spilling beer all over his T-shirt. "We just had to keep it on the down low because I was part of the crew and she was part of the cast. She was going to be the star of this season. But for appearances and ratings, it was best if everyone thought she was in love with that numbskull dolt Robbie Gibbons, but she loved me. And I loved her."

Dana and Benny gave each other puzzled looks. It seemed genuine to Dana, but then again he was stinking drunk, so she shrugged.

"You don't believe me either. No one does. Well, I don't care. I know the truth, and now everyone knows, so they fired me. Well, I'll show them. I'll show Robbie. I'll show you all," TJ said as he lumbered up to his feet, out of balance. He stood there for a few seconds like a man on a wire, but he eventually could stand somewhat erect, and he stumbled away, holding on to the bottle of beer like it was a ring buoy and he was lost at sea.

"Should we go after him?" Dana asked.

"He's two hundred and thirty pounds easy, and he's drunk and belligerent. We couldn't stop him if we wanted. He'll be fine. He just needs to sleep it off," Benny said.

"Look at this mess he left behind."

Benny sighed. "Darn tourists always leaving trash behind," he said as he kneeled down and began picking up the empty bottles TJ had left behind.

Dana joined in picking up empty bottles and their little tin caps. The bottles were sticky and caked in wet sand, and they smelled like warm leftover beer. So much for their quiet, romantic night stroll under the stars.

EIGHTEEN

The next morning, Dana drove down to Ark Row. She parked and walked to the bookstore slash cafe. The Ark Row merchants parked at the far end of where Ark Row began to leave the parking spots right in front of the stores to customers.

As soon as she could see her shop, she saw TJ pacing out front.

It surprised her to see him up that early in the morning, considering how drunk he had been less than ten hours ago.

She sighed, not being too keen on dealing with him or anyone from the television show. The cast and crew were turning out to be an insufferable bunch.

But it wasn't like he was giving her much of a choice, since he was loitering out front.

As soon as they made eye contact, he gave her a thin smile and a limp-wrist half wave. He was standing in front of the shop's door, blocking the entrance with his hefty frame, and he didn't move to give her access to her own store.

Is he waiting for me? Dana wondered.

"Hi, Dana. I'm TJ Summers," he said, sounding nervous. Dana chuckled, she remembered him. Although she hadn't known his last name until that moment. She was about to say that she knew who he was but he continued to speak, "I stopped by to talk to you, but Mindy said you don't come in until later, so I thought I would wait for you."

His appearance was a rumpled mess. He was in the same Iron Butterfly T-shirt and khaki cargo shorts that he had the previous night.

His clothing was dotted with stains from a night of heavy drinking on the beach and who knows where else. His disheveled hair and beard were all over the place. He looked like a street person off the streets of San Francisco. *I shouldn't be surprised*, Dana thought, *since he was so drunk the previous night*. But beyond his messy appearance on that morning, he looked downright terrified about something.

"Well, come on inside, I'll get you a cup of coffee on the house."

"Um, no thank you. I've already had three cups. And two of those delicious egg and chorizo bagel breakfast sandwiches." Thinking about Mindy's breakfast sandwiches seemed to bring some joy to the man, then his face turned back to panic.

"I just need to talk to you for a minute. About last night," he whispered the about last night part, and he looked around, making Dana look around too. Was someone watching them?

"Okay, shoot."

TJ looked around more and he got closer to Dana. He smelled terrible—a mixture of sweaty sea air, stale booze, coffee, and sausage. Spit it out so you can go take an hour-long shower, Dana wanted to tell him, but she stood there, looking at him with a puzzled look.

"First, I'd like to apologize to you and your friend. As you could tell, I was very drunk. So I'm sorry. But, I beg of you, please don't tell anyone about the stupid things I said last night."

"I'm surprised you remember," Dana said, smiling. TJ didn't smile, he just looked horrified.

She figured he wasn't in the mood to be teased about it. "Don't worry, what happens on the beach late at night stays on the beach," Dana said.

"Thank you. It's very important that you and your friend don't tell anyone about what I said about Rose Budd and me. You haven't told anyone, have you?"

"Nope. You're actually the first person I've seen this morning. So don't worry, I won't say anything."

"None of what I told you about me and Rose was true. Like she would have been interested in a slob like me," he said, looking down at his Birkenstocks.

"Don't be so rough on yourself, but don't worry. None of that is my or anyone else's business, so I won't say a word about it."

That seemed to lighten up the thousands of pounds of stress he seemed to have been carrying on his shoulders that morning.

"Can you also ask your friend not to say anything?"

"Don't worry, he won't, but I'll tell him. So how long is the production shut down for?"

"I don't know. The producers are fighting with the Costa Rican officials about it right now. Every day we're shut down, they're losing a ton of money. And we have deadlines in order to shoot enough footage to cut into a show in time for the season premiere in the fall."

"So you'll be sticking around?"

"Why wouldn't I?" he blurted, sounding defensive.

"You said they fired you last night."

"Oh, sorry. No, that was just a misunderstanding. Hopefully, we can get back to work soon. Besides, the cops said none of us can leave until they give us the okay individually, so even if

I wanted to go back home to LA, I can't. I'll be arrested at the airport."

"I guess they're conducting their investigation and they don't want potential witnesses to leave," Dana said.

"And suspects."

"What do you mean?"

"You said potential witnesses. Well, the cops are trying to find out who killed Rose, and if I had a dollar to bet, I would bet that Detective Picado thinks it was one of us from the show."

TJ seemed to hold back tears whenever he said Rose Budd's name.

"So you have met Detective Picado?"

"Unfortunately, I have. He's a tough son of a gun."

Dana laughed. "I must agree with your assessment."

TJ finally cracked a thin smile. "So you have met him too?"

"It's a small town, most of us have at one time or the other met with him." Dana didn't want to get into her personal history with Picado, so she left it at that.

He once again begged her not to tell anyone about their conversation last night or about what they had just spoken that morning. Dana reassured him for what must have been the fifth time. TJ finally seemed satisfied that she would keep their encounter last night to themselves.

"Okay, thank you," he said as he shuffled away down Main Street. Dana watched him for a moment, and he was heading towards the footpath. She figured he was staying at the resort like most of the cast and crew were doing.

Dana called Benny on her mobile phone. She was still standing out front, so she spoke quietly and told him about her encounter with TJ.

"It makes sense. No matter what the truth is about his relationship, he was talking out of school, which could jam him up with the police and his employer."

"Especially with the police, since significant others are usually prime suspects," Dana said.

"I'm sure Picado is on top of that if it's true, so let's not get involved further with TJ. The man could be dangerous."

He seemed harmless to Dana. She didn't see it as cut and dry as Benny usually saw things. She was not too worried about TJ, but it intrigued her. What was going on with him and on that show? Could he have really been dating Rose Budd? Seemed unlikely, but then again, Julia Roberts married Lyle Lovett.

Regardless, she had given him her word, and she would keep it even if she had a thought in the back of her mind niggling away at her. Maybe he was afraid and didn't want anyone to know about what he said on the beach because he was an obsessed stalker or a spurned lover that was dumped for Robbie Gibbons.

It was hard to fathom such scenarios. Unfortunately, there had been many dead women at the hands of an obsessed or spurned man.

She was all about keeping his secret to save him embarrassment or being fired, but she would not be manipulated into helping cover up his malfeasance in the death of Rose Budd. So she needed to look into the matter further. She wasn't about to throw him under the bus if what he had told her just now was the truth.

After hanging up with Benny, Dana walked into the store. Compared to yesterday, it was quiet. She realized then that the few minutes she had stood out front with TJ and then on the phone with Benny, not a single customer had entered the shop.

As soon as Dana stepped inside, Mindy was on her.

"Why was TJ so adamant to talk to you? He hung out there for an hour, waiting for you to arrive. It was freaky," Mindy said without even a good morning.

Leo popped his head from the kitchen. "Don't you worry, Dana, I had my eye on you two. If he tried anything..." Leo waved a bagel knife in the air.

"Settle down there, Rambo," Mindy said teasingly.

Dana laughed. "Thanks, Leo."

"Well, what did he want with you?" an impatient Mindy asked again.

"Oh, nothing, really. Benny and I ran into him last night during our walk on the beach. He was drunk, so he wanted to make sure he didn't say anything inappropriate and to apologize."

"He seemed like he had just woken up from a massive bender," Mindy said, looking out the window as if to make sure he was gone.

"He's gone, right?" Dana said, looking outside.

"Yes, he walked away onto the footpath," Mindy replied.

"He's probably staying at the resort," Leo said.

Dana had heard that the production company had blocked about thirty percent of the resort so that even when the production team and cast members were supposed to be filming on the island, they still had a place to stay while Picado investigated Rose Budd's death.

Dana couldn't imagine how much Gustavo Barca was charging for that, but the production company and the television network that ran the show had deep pockets.

But the work stoppage ordered by the police probably had them sweating bullets. Time is money, after all, and now everything had come to a screeching halt except for the money being spent by the studio on a show forced to stop shooting.

"Did he get out of line with you last night?" Mindy asked.

"Oh, no. I was with Benny anyway. He said nothing really, just talking drunken gibberish is all. He was just embarrassed, and he apologized."

"He seemed so nervous. He was here when I showed up to open up. At first I thought he was just eager for some coffee and food, but he asked where you were right away. He was acting strange, freaky. I was going to call you to warn you but then I got slammed with the door-opening morning rush."

"It's fine. He's harmless," Dana said, trying to sound like she believed it.

NINETEEN

Later that day in the afternoon, Russ Donnelly walked into Books, Bagels, and Lattes like he owned it.

Dana was in the bookstore side, going through inventory. She looked up when the door chime trilled and saw Donnelly walking towards her. He strutted like he was Tony Manero on a Brooklyn sidewalk. All that was missing was polyester clothing, for him to be holding a can of paint, and the Bee Gees belting out about staying alive on the stereo instead of the calypso/reggaeton/salsa fusion Mindy had on.

He flashed the same fake Hollywood smile she had been used to seeing when she lived in LA.

It was surreal for Dana to now see those same bright, white, toothy smiles all over Mariposa Beach along with other surgical augmentations.

It made her squirm. Come to think of it, Dana thought, he had flashed those bleached teeth the first time she had met him outside of the Qué Vista Restaurant when he was trying to contain the bad publicity Rose Budd and Robbie Gibbons were cooking up that night. It was the same smile. She wondered if he practiced it in front of a mirror. She assumed Russ Donnelly spent a lot of time gazing into mirrors, lost in his own big, bright blue eyes.

"I've been meaning to pay a visit to your establishment since I got back to town," he said. He stopped in the middle of the store and looked around.

"I believe this was a video store last time we were here for Season Nine. That must have been six or seven years ago."

"Good memory, Mr. Donnelly. This used to be the only video store in a fifteen-mile radius. It lasted longer, but it too went the way of Blockbuster," Dana said.

He smiled. More bleached teeth.

"I like this much better," he professed magnanimously. "And please, call me Russ."

Dana forced herself to smile, not really caring what he thought about her establishment or what he wanted her to call him. She realized that she didn't care much for him.

"What can I get for you?" she asked. There weren't any other customers in the store, so Mindy was in the kitchen, prepping for the mid-afternoon rush with Leo. Amalfi was manning the counter. The aroma of fresh pineapple and coffee permeated the entire store, and it smelled delightful—a bonus that Dana enjoyed after combining her bookstore with Mindy's cafe.

Dana looked him over with an equal amount of disdain and curiosity.

Russ Donnelly was in his early fifties, but he was fitter than most twenty-somethings. He was handsome, tanned, and a multimillionaire reality television powerhouse.

Dana had googled his net worth, and according to one of those websites that professes to know celebrities' net worth, he was worth a cool $300 million dollars. It was hard to fathom that the man standing right in front of her in her little shop in little old Mariposa Beach was so stinking rich and powerful.

He wore his thick mane of black hair combed back with just

the right amount of product to hold it in place without giving away that he had a product in there to do that. His entire bon vivant demeanor and attire—a $400 Versace polo shirt tucked into $500 Dolce and Gabbana drawstring-waist shorts, a $1,000 Versace messenger bag over his shoulder, and a $30,000 white gold Rolex perpetual chronograph watch wrapped around his right wrist—fit into the five-star luxury of the Tranquil Bay Resort a few miles up the mountainside, but he might as well be from another planet compared to the laid-back, sleepy town of Mariposa Azul Beach, which was more up to speed for bird watchers and beachcombers.

He oozed confidence, but he knew how to turn on the charm to get what he wanted from people he couldn't intimidate with his power or money.

Dana had had her fill of entitled rich men living in Los Angeles and San Francisco, and she didn't care about him or his television show. She figured he could sniff her contempt right off her, so he turned on the charm level with her high enough that the needle in her imaginary bull detector was bouncing into the thick cheesy zone.

"You opened this place by yourself?"

"I opened the bookstore, then Mindy moved her cafe here a couple months later."

"Very impressive. You moved into a new country. Different culture. And within months you're running your own business and you get the most popular eating spot in town to move in with you to boot."

"Is there something I can help you with?"

"Sorry. I'm a known ear-bender. I was in sales before getting into show business, so old habits die hard. I'm curious, are all your books for sale in English? Being that you're in a Spanish-speaking country and all."

"Actually, we have a Spanish section, but my target customers are American and Canadian tourists and the expats that are scattered up and down the coast and up the mountain. So the majority of my books for sale are in English. You're interested in buying a book?"

Donnelly picked up a copy of James Michener's *Hawaii* and whistled at the heft of the book, which had over a thousand pages. "Oh, I remember his books. They were the epitome of door stoppers."

"You like to read?"

"In another lifetime. Aside from scripts being pitched to me, I don't really have time for reading something like this beast," Donnelly said, putting the Michener book back on the shelf. "You know, we'll be back to shoot another season down here in a year or two, and I'm always looking for locals on the ground to help the production. Like your next-door neighbor, Big Mike. Maybe we can hire you as a consultant," Donnelly said.

"Thank you, but I had my fill from the whole LA scene."

"You lived in LA?" he asked, but Dana had the distinctive feeling that he had done his research about everyone living in town, so he already knew that. But he looked at her all quizzically, so if it was an act, he was just as good of an actor as he was a producer and studio executive.

"Something tells me you already know that," Dana replied with a grin.

His tanned faced betrayed a reddening. He put his hands up in the air in surrender.

"Guilty as charged. My research team is very good," he said.

"So what can I get for you, Mr. Donnelly?" Dana said, giving him a frosty look.

"Actually, can I speak with you... in private?" he replied, glancing over at Amalfi and Mindy.

Dana sighed. "Sure. We can talk in my office. It's in the back. Follow me. I'll be right back, Amalfi."

Dana walked into her office. She stood by the door as Donnelly went inside. She followed him and closed the door.

"Please, sit," she said, sitting down on the chair behind her desk. There were two guest chairs on the other side of her desk. Donnelly sat on the one to the right. He sat straight, with his feet firmly planted on the floor. Confident.

"Thank you for talking to me privately. As you can imagine, this whole situation with Rose Budd has brought on a lot of havoc to my life."

Dana was picking up a pattern talking with the likes of Dakota and Russ Donnelly. The death of Rose Budd was being a major inconvenience to their Hollywood life. How dare she get murdered? Such an inconvenience. Dana fought the urge to roll her eyes at the man.

"Okay," she said, not knowing what else to say.

"You and your friend had that unfortunate encounter with an inebriated Rose and Robbie, and it's my understanding you recently had an encounter with an even more inebriated TJ."

It surprised Dana. *He must have eyes everywhere up and down the coast.*

"What exactly do you want, Mr. Donnelly?" an exasperated Dana asked.

"Direct and straight to the point. So non-Hollywood, I love it. And please, like I said before, call me Russ," he said, smiling.

She glared at him.

"Okay, okay, I'll get to the point. I know this will come across rather crass, but I have a brand I need to think about and protect despite the terrible news about Rose. Over two hundred jobs are at stake. People only see the talent or the executive producers like myself involved in a television show and they think everyone is a fat cat millionaire, but most my staff are hardworking men and women that do the work behind the scenes such as camera operators, makeup artists, boom operators, location scouts, accountants, and such. Many people behind that curtain work in the non-glamour jobs we associate with Hollywood. And if this season is lost, so will a lot of jobs. And in a reality show, the talent are amateurs, trying to win the big prize or to catch a break with their modeling and acting careers," Donnelly said, maintaining eye contact with Dana the whole time.

"So you're worried that I'm going to talk about what I saw to TMZ?"

Donnelly laughed. "It has crossed my mind. The paparazzi are bottom feeders that pay for gossip to publish, and they're going to be all over this once word reaches Hollywood."

"Well, don't worry, Mr. Donnelly, I'm not planning on chatting with paparazzi." She refused to call him Russ.

"Great," Donnelly said, reaching into his expensive Versace messenger bag and pulling up a thin folder.

"I have two nondisclosure agreements for you and your friend to sign."

Dana was stunned. She felt ambushed. Then angry.

"I'm not signing anything right now. You can leave them with me and my friend, Benny, who is a lawyer, can look over them with me. And then I'll consider it. But I'll be honest with you, I'm not keen on signing any legal documents," she said. The whole thing sounded more absurd the more she thought about it.

If Donnelly was disappointed, he hid it well. His facial expressions and body demeanor didn't change one iota. He just smiled and told her he understood that and encouraged her to have it looked over by her attorney.

That said, he got up, shook her hand, and he opened the office door and walked out. Dana sat there for a moment, stunned. She composed herself and headed back to the shop. Donnelly was ordering a coffee to go from Amalfi. Dark roast. No sugar. No cream. Big-teeth grin shining bright.

TWENTY

Her encounter with Russ Donnelly and his nondisclosure agreement he wanted her to sign left Dana hot and bothered for the rest of the day.

Mindy and Leo were just as shocked as she was, and then Leo got plain angry. "He comes to our town, takes it over for a couple months, and now he wants to tell you what you can and can't say you saw on our public beach," Leo said, shaking his head.

"This looks scary," Amalfi said, reading the document. She quickly handed it back to Dana as if to not get infected with its bad juju.

Dana's emotion soon joined with Leo's. "Who does he think he is?"

"Someone who's worth multiple hundred million dollars and probably has an army of skivvy Hollywood attorneys at his beck and call. Be careful, Dana," Mindy said, sounding worried.

It was hard for all of them to carry on with business as usual for the rest of the day until closing time.

Dana had taken a picture of the agreement with her phone and sent it to Benny. He would look it over and they would talk about it when Dana got home. He agreed to meet her at Casa Verde at seven o'clock p.m. He told her he would bring dinner. Dana appreciated the gesture, since she was so upset about Donnelly's NDA that she had a hard time focusing at the shop. Dinner was the last thing on her mind. If it weren't for Benny's thoughtfulness, she probably would have had a piece of toast or something. The thought of eating made her queasy, but then she reminded herself it wasn't food making her feel that way—it was Russ Donnelly.

Benny arrived at 7:10 p.m. It was unusual for him to be late, but he told Dana that he drove up to Nosara to the only Chinese food restaurant nearby. Dana thought that was sweet of Benny, since he knew how much she liked Chinese food. And luckily for her, the only Chinese restaurant around, Dragón Trópico, was delicious. The food was good, but a little different from what she was used to in San Francisco. It was Chinese food with Costa Rican influences.

Dana had met the owner of the restaurant, Miguel Chen, when she attended her first Nosara District Chamber of Commerce meeting.

He was a tico through and through. He hardly spoke Chinese, much to the heartbreak of his ninety-nine-year-old grandmother, who had immigrated to Costa Rica when she was a child and her father joined his brother to work for the Panamá Canal Railway.

The family eventually settled in Puntarenas, where Miguel Chen was born and raised. Sensing a terrific opportunity to open the first Chinese restaurant in the Nicoya Peninsula, he moved to Nosara years ago, and his restaurant, located in downtown Nosara, had been going strong ever since.

Dana perked up when she saw Benny walking in with two white bags from Miguel Chen's restaurant.

"I went a little overboard," Benny announced, putting the bags on the kitchen counter.

The restaurant's logo was visible on the bags. It was a traditional Chinese dragon wrapped around a palm tree. Dana loved that branding.

Benny started to remove the ubiquitous Chinese food to-go boxes from the bags, revealing chow mein, pork fried rice, and a nice mix of dim sum: zongzi wrapped in a bamboo leaf, shrimp har gow, moo shu pork, and pineapple buns.

"Are we expecting more people?" Dana teased.

They ate for like ten minutes, chatting about other things and enjoying the food. Dana was glad she didn't settle for avocado toast.

She tried not to get into it right away, but Donnelly's NDA sat on the counter, mocking her. She was unable to ignore it any longer. "The nerve of the pompous blockhead," she blurted out, tapping on the NDA documents with her chopsticks.

Benny smiled. He picked up the NDA. "It's a whopper of a document he wants us to sign. It's very heavy-handed, even for an NDA."

"Can he really put that in there about not saying anything?"

"That's not uncommon, since this is a legal contract trying to get us to agree to keep what we saw and heard confidential. To not pass on that information to any third parties."

"I'm assuming he's worried we have TMZ on speed dial."

Benny laughed.

"So he is threatening to sue us from here to kingdom come if we tell anyone about Rose Budd and Robbie Gibbons's drunken brawl and TJ's drunken crying about his love for Rose?"

"Basically. He also wants jurisdiction for any legal matters related to the NDA to be in the United States. In Los Angeles County, not Costa Rica."

"Yeah, like I've been telling you, the nerve of that pompous pinhead."

"You said he was a blockhead before," Benny said with a smile. He was trying to bring some levity to the situation.

"Blockhead, pinhead, idiot, you get the gist."

"I do. Well, we're not signing it. That's for sure," Benny said.

"I'm glad you agree with me on that issue." It had worried Dana that Benny would push for them to sign the NDA.

As an attorney, he had the skill to look at things in a dispassionate way and decide based on sound legal footing, not letting emotions get in the way. And that was a good way to look at these types of things and why he was a successful lawyer, but Dana wore her heart on her sleeve and had heard more than a few times in her lifetime that she was as stubborn as a spotted mule.

Donnelly had tried to increase the odds of them signing the NDA by offering a big cash incentive in the amount of $15,000, which insulted Dana versus enticing her to sign.

"So if he's offering fifteen thousand dollars to each of us, he's probably doing the same to everyone else involved, like Maria and her staff at the restaurant, since they witnessed Rose and Robbie's public meltdown. And what about who was there for dinner? That's over one hundred thousand dollars, easy," she said, following it with a long, drawn-out whistle.

"It's a lot of cash to be throwing around over something that seems trivial," Benny said.

"Especially in his line of work. Stories of out-of-control reality TV stars make for good ratings, like that woman who flipped that table over in a restaurant a few years ago."

Even though both of them didn't watch that show, they both

remembered the table-flipping incident because the producers used the clip over and over to promote the show.

"What's he trying to hide?" Dana wondered.

"He has a dead cast member. One that appears to have been killed on set. You worked PR, he's probably trying to salvage the show and his reputation."

"These kinds of NDAs with this kind of hush money being tossed around town go beyond a regular PR campaign. Something happened on that island and now Russ is trying to cover it up."

"That's a lot of jumping to conclusions," Benny warned.

Dana shrugged, but she didn't reply. She knew it was the truth. Maybe not in Costa Rica, but in the States, companies didn't offer big-money NDAs unless there was something they wanted hushed up tight, and Dana would find out what Russ Donnelly wanted to hide so badly that he was willing to spend all that money.

"I know what you're thinking, Dana," Benny said, looking at her.

She smiled sheepishly. They were getting to know each other so well.

"What?"

"When you get all quiet like this, it usually means you will do something you shouldn't be doing. Dangerous stuff."

"Base jumping is dangerous. I'm not doing that, but I will try to find out what happened on the island and to Rose Budd."

TWENTY-ONE

The next morning, Dana was at the bookstore slash cafe. It was slow, as it usually got by ten o'clock a.m.

She kept looking out the window towards Big Mike's Surf and Stuff, which was located next door.

The last time she had talked with Big Mike, he told her how he had been hired as a consultant for the reality show. He had boarded Don Gerónimo's boat with the rest of the production crew and headed out to Santa Rita Island.

She assumed that since the production had come to a screeching halt because of Detective Picado's investigation, he would be back in town and in his store on that morning. She wanted to talk to him.

Carlitos Moreno, who worked for Big Mike, always opened the store at nine o'clock a.m. Big Mike usually arrived between nine thirty to ten o'clock.

At 9:46 a.m., she heard his car whirring by. Dana looked out the window to confirm it was Big Mike's orange 1970s Volkswagen microbus, which it was.

She wanted to bolt outside and run over to intercept him,

but figured she better check her craziness a bit and give him a few minutes to park, walk to his shop, and get settled in.

She went back into her office to bide time. After about five minutes of tapping her fingers on the desk, she figured that was more than enough time for Big Mike to get settled in, so she headed over next door.

Big Mike was talking with Carlitos when Dana walked in. "Hi, Big Mike."

He turned around and smiled. "Oh, hey neighbor."

"Can I talk to you for a minute?"

"Sure thing, give me a sec," he replied. He turned his attention back to Carlitos. "Okay, mate, finish up with the count. I'll be right back." He turned back to Dana. "Let's step into my humble abode," Big Mike said, pointing towards his back office.

Just like her shop, Big Mike's shop wasn't one of the original ark boats that were brought in from the water. Each of the merchant shop cottages had the same layouts, so Dana's store and Big Mike's store looked similar. Just like at her place, Big Mike had a private office in the back. Dana followed him there.

Big Mike was in his forties, but he was pushing twenty-one in his mind and in the way he dressed and talked.

As usual, he wore surfboard shorts, a T-shirt, and flip-flops. Come to think of it, Dana thought, she had never seen him wearing anything but shorts in the months since she had moved to town. The thought made her smile. He was such a free-spirited and kind man.

The only variance in his attire was the print on the T-shirt. On that day, he was wearing one of his custom shirts. Big Mike had an amazing drawing talent. Dana was certain he could have become a professional cartoonist had he not chosen the beach bum lifestyle. But then again, she couldn't imagine Big Mike in school or working for anyone but himself.

"Is that a new print?" Dana asked as she sat down. She was

eager to ask him about the show, but figured she'd be polite with a little chitchatting first.

She pointed at his T-shirt. It was the side view of a cool-looking sunglass-wearing toucan with a surfboard under its wing. The background was the red, white, and blue colors of the Costa Rican flag.

"Yeah, you like it?"

"I do."

"The tricky part was to draw the bird to not look like Toucan Sam so Kellogg can't sue me," Big Mike said, laughing. He had a wheezing laugh that reminded Dana of Muttley, the snickering dog from the Hanna-Barbera cartoons. But it was courtesy of his pack-a-day Delta cigarette addiction.

"Your bird is cooler than Sam, that's for sure," Dana said.

Big Mike's desk was made from old surfboards, and he sat on a large blue exercise ball, which he bounced on like a kid.

She sat on a papasan chair across Big Mike's desk. The large, bowl-shaped chair seemed an odd choice for an office chair, but she smiled because that was Big Mike... odd.

"What's up, D?"

"I was curious about what happened on the island with Rose Budd and the police shutting down the production."

Big Mike fidgeted on the big bouncy ball and he looked around nervously.

"The producers made me sign an NDA agreement when they hired me."

"I'm familiar with their NDAs. Russ Donnelly gave me one yesterday that he wants me to sign."

"Huh? Why is trying to get you to sign one? He hasn't hired you for anything, has he?"

"No. But I witnessed some appalling behavior from Rose Budd and her boyfriend. So I guess he's worried that I'm going to sell it to TMZ or something."

Big Mike seemed puzzled. "I can believe that you witnessed some bad behavior from Rose Budd. Not to talk ill of the dead, but boy, she was a mess, poor girl. But from her boyfriend... I can't believe it. TJ is a nice guy. A real straight shooter."

Dana felt like she had sunk in about ten feet deeper into the papasan chair, and her look must have showed her surprise, because Big Mike asked her, "What, girl?" It reminded her that she had a terrible poker face, so it was good she didn't like to gamble.

"I was talking about Robbie Gibbons. That's who she was having dinner and a nasty fight with. And she said it was her boyfriend."

Big Mike wrinkled his nose and shrugged.

"I take it that's news to you?"

"Yeah, well, she and TJ were all lovey-dovey, man. Sure, they were an odd couple—beauty and the schlub—but those two were in love."

Dana wasn't expecting to hear that from Big Mike, but perhaps he was reading into things. It's not like he really knew them, and he probably only saw them a handful of times during the week he worked for the production company before they shut it down, so how much could Big Mike really know about Rose and TJ?

"How can you be so sure?"

"I got tight with TJ, him being part of the crew and all, and that's where I was relegated to crew status. They kept the crew and cast separate. The producers wanted the cast to carry on like the crew didn't exist, since that made for better television. TJ would have been sent packing if Russ had found out about them two, so although they didn't hide it from the blue-collar crewmembers, they hid it from the producers, especially from Russ."

"How does Robbie Gibbons fit into all this, then?"

"TJ told me all about that. They manufactured it. Reality, my foot. Russ Donnelly is behind everything, pulling strings. He chooses the cast members. He decided who will last the longest and which cast member will be the star, the villain—all of that reality television stuff is all made up."

Dana didn't doubt that reality TV shows were baloney for a New York minute. And now she thought what TJ said the night before was the truth, not what he said the following morning.

It now made sense to her. After all, that was exactly what TJ had told her and Benny the other night on the beach. Then he showed up the next morning to walk back everything he said about him and Rose. Then Russ Donnelly showed up with his NDA.

He had seemed sincere in his heartbreak and sadness on that night, and the truth usually came out when a person was drunk—at least, some version of the truth.

It seemed plausible to Dana that Russ Donnelly forced TJ to lie, but why?

TWENTY-TWO

Dana walked out of Big Mike's store and started to walk back towards her bookstore slash cafe with her mind racing a mile a minute. What TJ had told her when he was drunk was the truth, and Russ Donnelly seemed determined to keep it a secret.

She had been so lost in thought that she didn't see that there was a person walking towards her until she bumped into him.

"Excuse me," she said before looking up and even knowing whom she had crashed into. She looked up, and it was Detective Picado. As usual, a scowl was present on his face.

"What were you doing at Mr. Pavlopoulos's store?" he asked, referring to Big Mike by his actual surname. He sounded angry.

Dana was taken aback by the question. *How dare he*, she thought.

"Excuse me?" This time she said it feeling insulted, not as an apology. He looked at her. "He's my retail neighbor, friend, and surfing teacher. We chat all the time," Dana replied, trying hard not to control her temper while Picado eyed her suspiciously.

"You have an uncanny ability to stick your nose into official police investigations. Getting into the middle of situations that do not concern you. I see you coming out of Mr. Pavlopoulos's store, him being a key witness, and I have to wonder if you're up to your old tricks again."

"You have some nerve," Dana said, and she stormed off.

She had her back to him as she made her way back to her shop, but she heard him talking towards her. "Stay away from my investigation or I'll have you detained for obstruction of justice." Dana stopped and turned to face Picado, who had said it loud enough for Big Mike to come out from his store just when she was about to go off on Picado.

"What's going on, man?"

"Same thing goes for you, Mr. Pavlopoulos. Don't discuss anything about this investigation with anyone," Picado turned to give Dana the stink eye, then he turned his attention back at Big Mike, "or I'll detain you for obstructing. Trust me. Neither of you will like Sebastián Prison."

Big Mike recoiled. Dana wasn't sure if it was from the threat or from being called Mr. Pavlopoulos, which he hated. He was just Big Mike.

It was Picado's turn to storm off, leaving Big Mike and Dana standing there, looking confused.

"What just happened?" Big Mike asked.

"He's a blowhard, that's all."

He scratched his long, stringy hair and shrugged, then he went back into his shop. Dana did the same.

Dana's encounter with Detective Picado left her shaken up, as usual, for the rest of the day. She was drinking coffee in her office when Mindy came in. "Heard the hubbub out there with Detective Picado," she said sheepishly.

"He's such a jerk."

"He is, but you better listen to him, honey. That man has it out for you since you got here with that ugly mess that went down during your inheritance fight and your cousin's murder. He'll lock you up on a three-month prevention hold just to get his revenge on you making him look bad during that investigation."

Dana sat back in her chair and sighed. She knew Mindy was right, and she held her hands up in surrender. "I know, I know. Benny tells me the same thing." She shouldn't be so stubborn, but she couldn't help it because her mom had told her she was since she was seven years old.

Mindy smiled. "It's because we care for you and don't want to see you get thrown in jail over something that really doesn't concern you, anyway."

Mindy smiled and headed back to the front lines to prepare for the mid-afternoon caffeine rush.

Dana sipped on her coffee. It was nice to have friends who cared for her, but as a former journalist, she had a lot of experience going up against intimidating people—far more intimidating than Picado—so he didn't scare her much. He just made her mad.

But deep inside, she knew Benny and Mindy were right. It wasn't her business to get into. She moved to Mariposa Beach to slow down, so she should do just that and live a more chilled life. She had enough to keep her busy with her bookstore to stick her nose where it didn't belong.

She had decided. She was done playing junior detective.

She had just processed that thought when she glanced at her computer monitor and the security video feed and saw Big Mike running into her store, frazzled.

She exited her office as she heard Big Mike calling her name loudly.

"What's going on?" Dana asked. Mindy, Leo, Amalfi, and several customers were all staring at the commotion.

"They arrested TJ."

TWENTY-THREE

Dana had always been a big-city girl. She was born in San Francisco. Like many San Francisco Baby Boomers, her parents fled down to the peninsula, where she grew up in San Mateo. And like many children of these San Franciscans in self-exile, she felt the urge to move back to the city her parents had left for the quieter suburbs.

After she was done with her college education, she was no different. She moved back to the city of her birth.

She had spent her adult life living in San Francisco and Los Angeles, where people kept to themselves, their eyes glued to their smartphones. All she knew about small-town life was what she had read about in books like Sinclair Lewis's *Main Street*. Like many San Francisco residents, she would escape the city up to the Sierra Nevada Mountain Range or camped out in the National Forests near the California–Oregon border. But she had never experienced small-town living, and she was amazed how similar things could be in the fictional small town of Gopher Prairie, Minnesota in the Sinclair Lewis book to the very real Mariposa Beach in Costa Rica.

It didn't matter that these were two very different countries

with their own cultures. A small town and its loose-lipped
people were similar, and word spread fast like a wildfire.

The news about TJ's arrest wasn't any different. Just about
everyone seemed to have their take on it.

"He was stalking that poor girl," Doña Amada, de facto
leader of the Gossip Brigade, had told Dana when she stopped
for coffee and a lox bagel.

"No, no, he made a move on her on the island, she turned
him down, he got furious, and killed her in a blind rage," fellow
gossip brigadier, Doña Evelyn, corrected her.

"Have they taken a good look at that truck driver that was
making deliveries to the restaurant?" Gerónimo Díaz asked.

"The one Dana saw on that morning she found the body?"
Dana heard someone else pipe in. Dana didn't even know who
that was or how they knew she had seen that delivery driver
with Julio at the Qué Vista Restaurant.

"Yes, him, he's from Nicaragua, you know," Gerónimo Díaz
replied ominously.

"Oh, the Nicaraguan boogeyman. You're awful, Gerónimo.
My grandfather was from Rivas," Álvaro López, an artist that
owned an art gallery a few doors down from the bookstore slash
cafe responded, sounding upset.

"Okay, everyone, we don't know anything for sure, and all
this speculating isn't doing any good, so let's not get too carried
away with our imagination," Mindy said loudly.

Dana was glad she was trying to nip the innuendo in
the bud.

"Besides, I heard it was just an accident. He didn't mean to
kill her," Doña Chilla added, as if Mindy had said nothing.

An exasperated Mindy rolled her eyes and sighed loudly.

"What about innocent until proven guilty?" Dana said out
loud to everyone that was going on about TJ killing Rose Budd.

There was silence for a moment, then a cackle of laughter.

"Oh, you idealistic Americans. In this country you're guilty until proven innocent." Doña Amada brayed with laughter.

Dana had gotten to know all about the differences in the judicial systems between the United States and Costa Rica.

She knew that in Costa Rica, if you were arrested, you did not have the presumption of innocence, and while it wasn't exactly "guilty until proven innocent" like Doña Amada claimed, the judicial system in Costa Rica was definitely set up to favor the prosecution, wherein in the States, the burden of proving guilt was on the prosecutor.

Another big difference in the two justice systems was that in Costa Rica, there was no bond system unless the court allowed it—which they rarely did—and that was done on a case-by-case basis, and it was solely up to the court's discretion. And in Costa Rica, the *fiscal*—the prosecutor—could request preventive detention while they built a case against you, which meant they could stick you in jail without officially charging you with a crime for months and even up to a year, even longer if the court allowed it. Once in jail under preventive detention, you couldn't bond out using a third-party bail bondsman like you could in the United States. You were stuck in jail. And it wasn't pretty.

Dana had learned that had happened to TJ: they arrested him on suspicion of killing Rose Budd, and since he was an American with a passport, they deemed him a flight risk, so he was placed under preventive detention.

"He's gone from the five-star Tranquil Bay Resort and fancy meals and on to the rice, beans, and chayote diet in San Sebastián," Doña Amada laughed.

Dana shook her head. They could be lovely ladies, but also so cruel. Mean girls at eighty. Dana knew what diet she was talking about. It was the standard meal prisoners of the infamous San Sebastián prison were fed. San Sebastián was in San

José, and it was the only prison that was used to hold those being held under preventive detention.

The prison was not dedicated to hold just those under preventive detention; it was a regular prison, so someone like TJ, who hadn't been charged with anything, could be in San Sebastián for months side by side with killers, drug dealers, and other violent criminals.

The prison was overcrowded, with most inmates sleeping on a thin piece of foam rubber on a dirty concrete floor.

Dana had to ask what chayote was the first time she heard about it. She learned it was a small, pear-shaped green tropical vegetable that was cheap to purchase and was available year-round. It was plentiful and cheap, a staple of prison meals, thus the chayote diet is what they called prison food.

Dana didn't like that kind of talk. For all any of them knew, TJ was innocent.

"I don't think it's funny," Dana said, wanting to throw them out of her bookstore slash café, but she knew the old ladies could be a handful, so she left before she said something she would regret.

Dana left Amalfi in charge of the bookstore. She needed to clear her head, so she jumped into Big Red and drove out to Benny's house.

Even though Dana had insisted he should go back to the city so as to not hurt his law practice, he had insisted on sticking around and had stayed three days longer than he had intended. But he needed to get back to the city, for he was due in court the next day, and it would be his weekend with his daughter, so he had to pick her up. He was packing when Dana arrived.

He offered her a soda, which she accepted as she told him about all the talk going on at the bookstore.

She couldn't get what was going on with TJ out of her head.

"It seems unfair to have TJ in that horrible jail without even charging him for any sort of crime," Dana said bitterly. She sounded bitter because she remembered back to when Detective Picado had threatened her with preventive detention during the investigation into her cousin's murder.

"I hate to say it, but the system is the system, nothing we can do about it."

"Can't you help him?"

"You know I don't do criminal law. What he needs is a good criminal lawyer to represent him, not a real estate attorney like me."

Dana took another sip from the soda and sighed.

She knew she was passively aggressively pouting, and she hated when she did that, but sometimes she couldn't help herself.

"I'll tell you what I'll do. When I get back to the city, I'll make some calls to see who's representing him, and maybe we can help him get a better lawyer."

Dana lit up and smiled. "Thank you."

"You're welcome, but it's probably a moot point anyway, since I'm sure Russ Donnelly is helping TJ because it looks bad on him to have one of his crewmembers killing a cast member. And he has more money than every single person in Mariposa Beach will see in their lifetimes, combined. So I'm sure he'll get him a top-notch attorney."

Dana wasn't so sure about that, but she wanted to think positive.

"I hope you're right."

"I won't get back to the city until this evening. I'm having dinner with my daughter, and I have to go to court tomorrow at ten, so I probably won't be able to look into this right away, but I promise you I will as soon as I can."

Dana smiled. She knew he would. When he said he would do something, it was like money in the bank.

They said their goodbyes, since she wouldn't see him until the weekend. This was the part of the long-distance relationship that she hated.

She was also nervous because Benny was bringing his daughter down for the weekend. The two of them got along well, but she was still nervous that she could turn at any moment and hate her like the horror stories she had heard from friends who had dated men with children.

Benny got into his SUV and drove off towards the highway. Dana was driving Big Red, heading back to town. She stopped at Soda Linda, which was located off of Main Street, about half a mile away from the shops of Ark Row. Sodas in Costa Rica were small, open-air cafes that were located in just about every town in the country regardless of its size.

It was where you experienced traditional Costa Rican food at its best.

Soda Linda had a limited menu and limited seating, but the food was delicious. Aside from the traditional gallo pinto and casado, the no-frills soda also offered a mean four-cheese grilled sandwich and arreglados—a refried bean and ham sandwich with cheese, Salsa Lizano, and lettuce and tomato that was Dana's favorite and what she ordered for lunch.

The place reminded Dana of a '50s American diner, with its long sit-down counter with direct service by the owner, Linda Orozco.

The soda was a family business. Linda usually had one of her two sons or her daughter-in-law working there. Dana hadn't met her husband, nor was he ever mentioned, so she assumed he was out of the picture, although she didn't dare ask about such personal matters. She figured eventually either Linda would tell her about it or someone from the Gossip Brigade would do the honors.

There were only nine stools on the other side of the counter, so during its busy time, you would have to order your food to go if you didn't want to wait around for a spot to open at the counter. Since it was past two in the afternoon, there were plenty of spots. Dana sat down, putting her keys, sunglasses, and her Kindle on the counter.

Linda greeted her warmly. Her son Oscar was working the grill; he waved before turning his attention back to the grill.

"Did you hear they arrested that poor girl's killer?" Linda asked her right away.

Dana smiled. The town was abuzz with the news all right, and there was no escaping it.

"It's the hot topic over at the bookstore. The Gossip Brigade is debating several theories why he might have done it," Dana said facetiously.

"Figures they would be the first to know and to tell everyone about it by noon," Linda said with a grin.

"To be honest, I feel bad for the guy. I talked with him a couple times, and I know that doesn't mean much, but he didn't seem like a killer to me, and now he's locked up in that horrible jail in San Sebastián without even being charged for anything yet."

"Well, the fiscal is working on it. I'm sure they wouldn't have arrested him if they weren't sure he did it."

Dana shrugged. Years ago, she used to sound that naïve about the justice system until her years working as a journalist opened her eyes to the fact that the judicial system failed and innocent people got locked up for years, even decades.

Dana ordered lunch, an arreglado and mango juice.

She was lost in thought as she waited. She had that feeling deep down inside that TJ didn't kill Rose Budd. She wanted to find out if TJ really was the killer. But how?

TWENTY-FOUR

After her late lunch, Dana returned to the bookstore just in time for the three o'clock p.m. caffeine rush.

With the production crew still on idle and off the island, it was busier than usual for the time of the year. By five o'clock, things quieted back down again as they prepared to close for the day in about an hour.

Dana was mulling over what to do about TJ. She could hear Benny and her best friend, Courtney, who was back in San Francisco, in her head, telling her it wasn't her concern and to not get involved. But if she were locked up unjustly, she hoped someone would help her, or at the very least check in on her.

"Everything okay, hon?" Mindy asked. That broke her out of her mini-trance. She realized she had been wiping down the same spot on the counter for a while.

She blushed. "Yes, sorry, just lost in thought."

"I could tell you were far, far away from here," Mindy said with a smile.

The door chime trilled, and in walked Detective Gabriela Rojas. She smiled at her warmly. Dana smiled back, but she also felt her body getting tensed up, since usually when Rojas was around, that meant Picado was nearby. She looked around for him but was happy to not see him.

Rojas ordered a skim latte and a fruit cup. She walked over to the bookstore side towards Dana.

"Where's your partner?" Dana asked as she got closer.

"He's at the Tranquil Bay Resort. We were interviewing witnesses. He's still up there doing some paperwork. I had some downtime, so I came down here. Mr. Barca says we can eat and drink anything we want for free during the investigation, but that seems unethical to me, especially with his reputation for shady deals. Besides, it's too ritzy and stuffy up there anyway, so here I am."

"Good choice. Hang out with us little people versus the hoity-toity ones," Dana said, smiling.

While Rojas waited for her order, Dana figured she would take the advantage of being able to talk with Rojas without having her surly partner there to tell her to butt out.

"Word around town is that TJ was sent to San Sebastián prison under preventive detention," Dana said quizzically.

Rojas turned to look at her with her eyebrows arched.

"It just goes to show that you shouldn't believe everything you hear, especially from gossipy busybodies who don't know what's what."

"So he's not at San Sebastián?" Dana said, sounding excited.

"Not yet. He's in one of the OIJ holding cells in Nicoya. The prosecutor has requested a three-month preventive detention, but it hasn't been reviewed by the court, so until then, he's in the holding cell, which is nothing like San Sebastián."

Dana felt relieved.

"How long does that process take?"

Rojas shrugged her shoulders as Mindy brought her coffee and fruit cup. Rojas thanked her as Mindy joined the conversation.

"Days. Weeks. Depends," she finally replied.

"I know you can't talk about the case much, but do you really think TJ Summers killed Rose Budd? Is the evidence that overwhelming to get him locked up?"

Rojas fidgeted a bit. Dana could tell her question made her uncomfortable. She took a sip from her latte.

"This is just between us," Rojas said, looking at Dana then at Mindy.

"Of course," they both said in unison.

"The case is strong. There was some DNA evidence that linked him to Ms. Budd, but he insists it's because they were boyfriend and girlfriend. And that seems to be true from our interviews with other crewmembers, but Mr. Donnelly insists that's not the case. So it's premature to arrest him, but I'm not the lead investigator in this case, Detective Picado is, and he had him arrested, so that's that."

"Do you think I could visit TJ?" Dana asked.

Rojas and Mindy both gave her a side-eyed glance.

"Why? You hardly know him," Mindy asked.

"I don't know. I feel bad for him. I realize I don't really know him from Adam, but I just can't believe he could have killed her or anyone, really. I remember how scared I was when Picado was threatening me with preventive detention a few months ago. So I don't know. I just want to visit him to let him know he hasn't been forgotten by the outside world."

"You realize Detective Picado would hit the roof if you visit Mr. Summers," Rojas said.

It was Dana's turn to shrug.

"It's not against the law, is it?"

"No, it's not against the law for you to see him. But he has to agree to see you."

"I might drive up to Nicoya, then," Dana said.

"Just remember this conversation is between us. Last thing I need is for Picado to think I encouraged you to go visit TJ," Rojas said.

"Don't worry, mum's the word."

Rojas smiled, took her coffee and fruit cup, and sat at a table by the window.

"I don't think it's a good idea for you to see him," Mindy said, sounding concerned.

"It will be fine. I'm also just curious about the judicial process here and seeing the OIJ offices. I guess my old reporter curiosity has kicked into high gear."

Dana got home at six thirty p.m. She knew Benny, Mindy, and oh, boy, her mother, and also her BFF Courtney back in the States would do a Captain Picard facepalm if they knew she was planning to visit TJ at the holding cell in Nicoya, but she didn't care.

She needed to get TJ's side of the story and to find out if Russ Donnelly was helping him out of the jam he was in, because she did not believe he was the killer. So instead of relying on hearsay, town gossip, and innuendo, she would get her information right from the source first thing in the morning.

TWENTY-FIVE

Nicoya was located about an hour north from Mariposa Beach. It was a city on the Nicoya Peninsula and the district seat of Nicoya cantón—county.

It was one of the country's most important tourist zones, serving as a transport hub to all the Guanacaste Province's beaches and national parks. It was also home to the closest OIJ substation to Mariposa Beach.

She left Casa Verde at eight o'clock a.m. and made the trip in an hour.

Even though Nicoya was the biggest town in the district and it looked huge compared to tiny and sleepy Mariposa Beach, it was still small, with a population of around twenty-five thousand.

She drove into town and to the OIJ police substation.

She parked out in front and looked at it in disbelief. It didn't look like the police stations she was used to back in the States. It looked like the property had been built as a residential home that was then converted to be a police station.

The property had a cream-colored exterior and a red roof. A white iron fence surrounded the building, and there was a small plastic blue sign that hung out in front that was swaying in the wind. The signage said: Subdelegación Del OIJ—Substation of the OIJ—in a bright white font.

She heard a rumbling in the sky and looked up. It seemed like Mother Nature must have been in agreement that it was a bad idea for her to be there, because just as she reached for the door handle to exit her Jeep, she unleashed a torrential downpour of biblical proportions.

"Great," Dana said out loud as she looked out the window. The sound of rain falling on the Jeep's canvas soft top sounded like she was being pelted with rocks. She looked at her small umbrella and laughed. "A lot of help you'll be," she said to it as she dropped it onto the floor.

She contemplated taking the omen and heading back home, but she was right there, so what the heck.

She exited Big Red and made the mad dash inside.

Although it took mere seconds to run from her vehicle to the OIJ station, she was drenched like she had just come out of a pool.

She was trying to dry herself like a shaking dog when a uniformed policeman with Fuerza Publica, the uniformed National Police force, looked at her and smiled. He handed her some paper towels. She thanked him and began to pat herself dry as best as she could.

"How can I help you?" the police officer asked while she was in mid pat.

"I'm here to visit TJ Summers, who I've been told is being held here," she said, still patting herself dry.

The helpful officer's smile turned to a frown right away.

"One minute," he said as he wandered off to the back of the station.

A couple minutes later, the police officer returned with

another uniformed cop and another one in civilian's clothing, who Dana assumed was a detective.

She was right. He introduced himself as Detective Granados. He didn't share his first name with her, and he began to pepper her with questions right from the get-go. He asked her who she was, what was her relationship with the prisoner, and why she wanted to see him.

Dana answered his questions. She told him she was a friend and just wanted to see how he was doing.

The detective looked at her suspiciously for a moment then told her to wait in the lobby, which she did.

The detective was gone for over ten minutes. She was worried that he was calling Picado, who would show up to yell at her and somehow prevent her from seeing TJ, but finally he returned by himself.

"Mr. Summers will see you. Come with me."

Dana followed Detective Granados to the back of the station. There were a few desks, and a couple detectives were on their computers. She didn't know how big the substation was, but if she had to guess, she would say there couldn't be over ten detectives working there at one time. She wondered which of those desks belonged to Picado and Rojas.

Granados brought her to a conference room and told her to sit and wait. She did as she was told and waited for fifteen minutes before finally the same uniformed police officer who had given her the paper towels to dry off walked in alongside TJ.

TJ's face lit up when he saw her. It surprised her to see that he wasn't handcuffed, and he was wearing his own clothing. Unless the OIJ was issuing T-shirts with Gene Wilder as Young Frankenstein with It's Alive in huge white font as its jail garb.

She expected for him be in an orange jumpsuit in leg and waist chains.

"Detective Granados has allowed for a ten-minute visit," the police officer said as he left the conference room and closed the door.

Dana had talked to TJ three times in her life, but he greeted her like they had been childhood friends or as if they were family.

"Thank you for visiting. I'm trapped in a living nightmare," he said as they both sat down at the table.

"What happened?"

"That Picado became convinced that I killed Rose, and he zeroed in on me and he was like a dog with a bone with me being the darn bone!"

"What you told me and Benny that night on the beach when you were drunk, that was the truth, wasn't it?"

He nodded his head slowly, his brown eyes tearing up. "I loved her. And I know it's hard to believe, but Rose loved me too."

"I believe you. But why all the cloak and dagger about you two?"

"All of us crewmembers signed NDAs and contracts prohibiting fraternizing with cast members. The cast members had to do the same thing. So we were both in violation of our contracts, so we had to keep it a secret. After Rose's death, it gutted me. And I drank too much, as you saw that night on the beach. The next morning, Russ called me into his hotel room for a meeting. He asked if it was true that Rose and I had become romantically involved. I told him it was true. He was very upset. Then he asked if I had told anyone outside of the production team. I said yes, to you two guys on the beach. I told him I was drunk. That made him even madder. He was livid. I had heard he had a terrible temper, but I had never witnessed it until that day, and it was scary. He yelled at me and then he threatened me, saying he would sue me for violating my contract and that he would blacklist me so I could never work in the entertainment business again. It terrified me. So he told me the only way to avoid that was to find you and take back what I had told you on the beach. And I felt like such a coward, but I did it."

"You're not a coward, you had to do whatever you could to protect your livelihood. It's understandable, especially since you were grieving."

"Still felt like I was turning my back on Rose."

Tears welled up in his eyes and started to trickle down his chubby cheeks and down his scruffy beard.

"Who do you think killed Rose?"

He sniffled a bit and swallowed hard, like he was trying to take back the tears.

"Believe me, I've thought about that a lot, but I don't know. The producers whip up the cast members to have beefs with each other so there were some nasty fights, but you never know if it's real or just put on for the camera."

"Who was she beefing with?"

"Robbie Gibbons. You saw that in real time that night at the restaurant when they got into an argument. He's a jerk and all, but I can't imagine him hurting her. He's too much into himself and what the show will do for his modeling and acting career."

"Who else was she beefing with?"

"Arianna Layton. They were at each other's throats, much to Russ Donnelly's delight," TJ said with contempt. He suddenly had a look like he had an epiphany. "Russ Donnelly," he said slowly.

"What about him?"

"He could have killed her. He has a nasty temper and a God complex. She had a huge falling-out with him."

"I thought he was setting her up to be the breakout star of this season?"

"Yes, but she wouldn't kowtow down to him. Drove him

nuts. So one second he's telling her he was going to make her the star of the show and then the next thing he was putting her down all the time. Telling her she had to lose weight before they started to film, that he should send her packing right away, just being mean and nasty towards her. Then he seemed to gravitate towards Arianna Layton and Dakota Hunter as his breakout star instead of Rose, which is one of the reasons she and Arianna began to hate on each other."

Dana remembered Dakota from that day in her cafe. It was the day Picado shut down the production of the show and the cast and crew arrived back on shore. TJ had been short with her for being too chatty in line and had seemed irritable, and it made sense to her now why he was lashing out. The woman he loved was dead, murdered, and he was being forced by Russ Donnelly to carry on as if she was just another cast member.

"Has Russ hired a top-notch lawyer to defend you?"

TJ scoffed. "I haven't seen or heard from Russ at all. It's like he has washed his hands of me. I've been told that the Costa Rican courts will appoint a public defender for me. And that's about all I know. This is crazy, they want to lock me up for three months of preventive detention. I haven't even been charged with anything, but they will lock me up and transfer me up to that horrible prison while they investigate, and Russ won't return my calls. I'm all alone."

It shocked Dana. She had assumed as Benny had told her that Russ would be hiring a hotshot attorney from the capital to represent TJ.

"What about the US Embassy? Aren't they helping?"

"They're useless. I had an embassy official by the name of Adam Mitchell call me after they arrested me," TJ said.

Dana remembered meeting Adam Mitchell when her cousin was killed, and he was pretty useless, since there wasn't much the American embassy could do when one of their citizens was arrested. They had to abide by the laws of that country, not the US.

"I met him once," Dana said.

"Well, he told he would visit me when I transferred up to San Sebastián to make sure I'm doing okay. I told him I was not doing okay, and to get me out of here, but they said their hands are tied. They have to abide by Costa Rican law. It's like I'm in a Kafkaesque nightmare. Please help me, Dana. I didn't kill Rose, I loved her."

The rain was still coming down in sheets as Dana made the mad dash again back to Big Red.

She sat in the car for a few minutes. She didn't bother drying herself off. She felt terrible for TJ. His mother couldn't afford to come down for a visit, and Russ Donnelly was ghosting him. He was alone in a foreign country, and she was convinced he had nothing to do with Rose Budd's murder.

She fired up Big Red and began to drive back down to Mariposa Beach. The rain was coming down so hard that the little wiper blades of the Jeep Willys had a hard time keeping the windshield clear. The water was seeping into the sides of the soft-top cover—a reminder she needed to get a wet-season car with a hard top.

Every mile she drove closer to home, the stronger her resolve to help TJ became.

She had her own ideas about who she needed to talk to, and by the time she drove into town, she knew she would check things out for herself. And she needed to get started right away because TJ didn't have much time before the police transferred him to that horrible prison in the city.

TWENTY-SIX

Dana got home soaking wet and cold. Wally sauntered over towards her, and when he saw her dripping wet, he ran back in the other direction as far away from her as possible.

"Oh, thanks for the support, you brat," she yelled out to him as he vanished around the corner.

She made her way upstairs, peeling off her wet clothing along the way. By the time she reached her bathroom, she had taken off her wet clothing. She wrapped a towel around her body and began to draw a bath. She turned the faucet in the bathtub on and wiggled her fingers under the stream of water until she had the right temperature flowing.

While the tub filled with hot water, she added Epsom salt and a soothing lavender oil to the water.

She lit a Zen soothing lavender candle that she had bought from the Pancha Sabhai Institute, a yoga retreat near her property on the same footpath that led up to the resort. The candles were handmade, and they were a delightful bliss during a nice, warm bath.

Next up in her bath routine, she put her Kindle e-reader into a plastic food storage bag. She was about to finish the Sue

Grafton novel. She had everything set how she liked it. She dropped the towel on the floor and lowered herself gently into the tub.

She couldn't help but moan out loud as she settled in and relaxed. Once he determined it was safe and that the bath being drawn wasn't for him, Wally carefully walked into the bathroom, since for whatever reason water to the silly kitty was like exposing a vampire to the sun. He stepped on the towel on the floor and began to knead it like a baker kneading dough, then he circled it about five times before he deemed it was worthwhile for him to lay down on it. Dana never grew tired of watching Wally's comfort rituals. She laughed and lowered herself further down into the lovely warm water.

She didn't end up reading her novel or doing much of anything else but just enjoyed the soothing stillness and quietness of her bath. Her mind had been spinning like a top thinking about TJ, and if she was right and he was innocent, who had killed Rose Budd and why?

She took a longer than usual bath. She looked at her pruned fingertips and flinched. "Oh, my, I need to get out of this tub," she said out loud to Wally, who was still snoozing on the towel. She got up from the tub and made her way out, splashing drops of water onto the floor, which sent Wally running out of the bathroom as if she had splashed him with hot oil.

She put on her robe and dried her hair, which was a much easier process after she had made the then frightening decision to cut her shoulder-length hair into a pixie cut a couple months ago.

She had felt sick to her stomach when she made the trip to a top salon in Escazú, but the hairdresser, whose name was Mauricio, made her feel at ease and he had done a marvelous job, and after all that fear and angst leading up to the haircut, she now just loved it. She liked how she looked with it, and it was so much more practical when living in the hot, humid, salty, dusty tropics of the Pacific coast.

After dressing, she made her way to the bookstore slash cafe in time for the noon rush. Although it wasn't raining as hard, it was still coming down, so business was steady but slower.

After the rush subsided, Mindy peppered her with questions about her visit to TJ in jail. Dana told her about seeing him and how he maintained his innocence and how Russ Donnelly was not helping him.

"The court will assign him a lawyer," Mindy said.

"Benny told me that. He's also making some calls to find him a criminal attorney that might do a better job than a public one."

"TJ is lucky you're in his corner," Mindy said.

"Why are you in his corner?" Leo said from the kitchen, startling them both.

"I didn't know you were eavesdropping," Mindy said to her husband, who just shrugged his shoulders.

"I don't think he did it, and no one is helping him, so I'll do what I can to help him out, since what he's going through almost happened to me just a few months ago."

Dana spent a quiet evening at home with Wally. She had a grilled cheese sandwich for dinner and a glass of red wine.

She could finally get into the Sue Grafton novel she had been reading without having thoughts of Detective Picado, TJ, and Rose Budd in her head.

At bedtime, she had some lavender tea, which was a perfect relaxing way to ease into sleep after a stressful day.

It worked, because she had a good night's sleep, waking up in the morning to find that Wally had made the move from the bottom of the bed to the top, where he had curled up into a ball of white fur by her head. She was a light sleeper, but she slept through Wally's journey from lying by her feet to ending up sharing her pillow. For the first time since she found Rose Budd's body, she didn't have any nightmares. And if the howler monkeys went wild that night, she didn't hear any of it.

She made her way downstairs. She had a glass of freshly squeezed orange juice and went through her morning coffee bean-grinding routine that she went through every morning. The coffee maker did its magic, and the house smelled of delicious coffee. She was convinced the coffeemaker was one of the greatest inventions in mankind. Forget the wheel.

The rains usually didn't start until the late afternoon, so she thought about going on a run.

She wasn't ready to run back towards the rock where she had found the poor mangled body of Rose Budd. She had other running routes to avoid the rocks. But she decided that it didn't feel as if she had a run in her that morning. Besides, she wanted to look into who could have killed Rose.

It was not as if TJ had a lot of time to spare before his transfer to the San Sebastián prison.

She called Benny to let him know that Russ Donnelly wasn't offering any legal help for TJ and he was going to be stuck with a public defender if they didn't help him.

"Wait a second, how do you know Russ Donnelly isn't helping him? Did you run into him in town?"

Confession time. "No. I talked to TJ and he told me."

"How did you... did you drive up to Nicoya to visit him?"

"Yes, I went there yesterday morning. The poor guy is all alone and terrified that the court will approve the three-month detention and he'll be transferred to prison."

"You could have told me you wanted to visit him and we could have gone there together when I was back in town."

She could hear it in his voice that he wasn't happy that she had gone up there. And it ticked her off a little. She was used to living in San Francisco and had been to worse places than an OIJ holding cell in Nicoya. She was thirty-five years old. She wasn't a spring chicken that needed protection like a delicate flower. But she knew he meant well and cared for her, so he worried. His chivalry was sweet and annoying at the same time. *Is that possible?* she thought. *Yes,* she answered to herself.

"He doesn't have that much time, Benny. As soon as the judges approve the preventive detention, they're transferring him."

Benny tried to speak, but Dana cut him off. She told him she was fine. That if she could handle interviewing Edmund Kemper, the so-called coed killer, at the state prison in Vacaville, California and dangerous MS13 gangbangers in San Quentin when she was a reporter for the *San Francisco Star,* that she could handle TJ in a holding cell in Nicoya with her eyes closed.

He backed off, knowing he was beat. The tiff was brief. She figured Benny knew she was right and that TJ needed help. Benny wasn't all the way on board with team TJ like Dana was, but he had promised her he would help her find a good lawyer for TJ, especially now knowing that Russ Donnelly had left him twisting in the wind and that the US Embassy was in spectator mode.

After her call with Benny and drinking her second cup of coffee, she walked down to her bookstore slash cafe and took her chances with the rain.

She arrived at Books, Bagels, and Lattes at eight thirty a.m.

As usual, Amalfi and Mindy were working the front and Leo was in the back kitchen.

There were only a couple people in line, with a few customers sitting on the bookstore side of the cafe where Dana had placed several big, comfy reading chairs and a couch. She opted not to put a communal table for laptop-toting customers. She wanted to create a comfortable spot to read while drinking coffee and eating a bagel purchased from Mindy, but she didn't want to give the illusion the bookstore was a library. Just a nice air-conditioned spot to enjoy good books, coffee, and great bagels and empanadas. Sales of books shot up after she made the change, so she was happy she did it. Mindy loved it too, since at her old place, the biggest complaint was there wasn't a place to sit and enjoy the coffee and treats.

As soon as Dana walked into the shop, Mindy went straight for her. "My, oh, my, you've been a popular girl this morning," she whispered.

"I have?"

"Russ Donnelly stopped by looking for you about an hour ago. Very pushy and smarmy, that one."

"Sounds about right. What did he want?"

"To talk to you. He said it was very important. I told him I didn't know when you would be in. He asked for your cell phone number and home address. I told him to go fly a kite, twice."

Dana smiled. They always had each other's backs. "Thank you."

"He got all Arnold Schwarzenegger and told me 'I'll be back.'"

Dana couldn't help but laugh out loud. "No, he didn't say that."

"Well, not in those words exactly, but the attitude was all Terminator-like."

"If the Terminator looked like an over-tanned George Hamilton," Dana nipped. They shared a laugh over that.

"But wait, there's more," Mindy said, recovering from the laughter. "Detective Picado was also looking for you about fifteen minutes ago. He seemed more huffy and puffy than usual. I told him what I told Russ Donnelly, so he said he would drive up to your house."

"I walked down the footpath this morning, so I must have missed him on the main road. Too bad," Dana said with a smirk.

"So what's going on, Dana? You seemed to have ticked both of them off."

"I went to visit TJ Summers yesterday at the jail in Nicoya."

Mindy took an actual step back. "Why?"

"I don't think he killed Rose Budd. I think he's being railroaded and they're pinning the murder on him."

Mindy looked at Dana with the same concerned look her mom gave her all the time.

"Dana, Detective Picado is a lot of things that make him a very unpleasant man to be around, but he's not going to send an innocent man to prison."

"I'm not saying he would do that on purpose, but he might be being used to do just that. Innocent people end up in prison more than you think."

"Why would anyone want to do that to TJ?"

"I don't know, but Russ Donnelly comes to mind."

"Okay, same question, why would he want to do that?"

"I don't know, but I will find out."

TWENTY-SEVEN

Dana was certain about one thing: she needed to talk to the cast members that seemed to be interwound with Rose Budd the most—Arianna Layton, Dakota Hunter, and Robbie Gibbons.

Those were the three cast members whose names kept popping up every time.

The cast members had been keeping a low profile since the production shoot was shut down by Detective Picado.

They were in limbo with nothing but time on their hands.

Aracelly Trejos was an assistant manager at the resort. She was Claudio Villalobos's girlfriend. Claudio was Ramón and Carmen's son who had worked at the resort and had been Dana's eyes and ears inside. But he had recently taken a better job at the Four Season Hotel in the Papagayo Peninsula, which was almost three hours away from Mariposa Beach.

Aracelly also disliked Gustavo Barca and her immediate bosses at the resort, and she really liked Dana.

She knew all about Barca wanting to buy Casa Verde so he could bulldoze it to the ground, leaving her boyfriend's parents homeless. So when Dana called her, she was happy to help.

Dana asked her if the cast members were still at the resort and what did they do all day with the production shut down.

She responded that they were staying at the resort and they spent the time lounging by the pool, hitting the resort's fitness center, playing golf, tennis, and annoying the staff with their entitled demands to be treated as if they were A-list stars.

She noted that they didn't seem to journey much outside the walls of the luxurious Tranquil Bay Resort.

Dana figured there was no need for them to go down to Mariposa Beach and mix with the plebs like her when they were being waited on hand and foot at the five-star resort.

Dana sent Aracelly a text asking her if the cast members were around.

Aracelly texted back right away that several of them were hanging out at the pool.

She left the bookstore slash cafe and began to walk towards where she usually parked Big Red, but remembered she had walked down that morning. So she turned back and began to power walk back to Casa Verde. She punched in the code to open the side door onto her property and was startled to see Ramón standing nearby, calling for her. She waved and he rushed on over.

"Detective Picado with the OIJ was here looking for you," Ramón said, wide-eyed.

"I know, it's okay," Dana said as she made her way towards her front door. Ramón followed her. "He was mad," Ramón said, sounding worried. "He saw your Jeep parked there and thought I was lying, that you were inside, but I told him you walked down to town."

That annoyed Dana. He showed up unannounced, so she

wasn't about to worry about Picado. If he wanted to talk to her so badly, he had her phone number. But she didn't want to talk about that with Ramón.

"It's okay, don't worry, I'll talk to him later." But he still looked worried. Dana smiled and repeated it again. "It's fine, don't worry, Ramón."

He didn't seem convinced, but he turned around and walked back towards the garden with his trusty machete dangling from his right hip.

Dana's hand had barely touched the handle to her front door when her mobile phone rang. She glanced at the screen and recognized the number: it was Picado.

Speak of the devil, she thought. She wasn't in the mood to be lectured or yelled at, so she ignored the call. She was sure all he wanted to do was to chastise her for visiting TJ even though she was well within her legal rights to do so.

She would avoid his calls and deal with him later. Way later.

She walked inside as Wally came prancing out from who knows where he was sleeping. He rubbed up against her leg as usual, and yawned, as usual.

"Sorry, Wally, just here to get Big Red's keys." She bent down and gave him a quick pet.

"I'll tell you what, I'll give you some of that good stuff you love. You won't even miss me." Dana walked into the kitchen and opened a drawer, and Wally knew what she was going for and he began to meow and purr so loudly, it rang her ears. He then stood on his hind legs with his two front paws kneading into Dana's legs gently.

Dana laughed. "I don't know, Wally, I think you might have a problem," she said as she pulled out a plastic sandwich bag stuffed to the brim with catnip.

Just like about everything in Casa Verde, the catnip was

home grown. Once Wally came crashing into her window late at night the first week she had moved in, giving her and her best friend Courtney a heart attack, and made himself at home, he had quickly won everyone over, including Ramón and Carmen. Ramón with his green thumb planted some catnip in the garden and it grew like crazy.

After catching Wally rolling around several times in the catnip plants, Ramón had to put a little protective mesh over them. Ramón would then snip the leaves and he would cut and grind them into the green pixie dust that put Wally into la-la-land.

Dana took two big pinches of the stuff and sprinkled them on the floor. Wally dove into the catnip like a hog to mud.

"Geez, Wally, I think I'm going to have to send you to catnip rehab," Dana said, laughing as she left Wally rolling around in the catnip, purring loudly.

Fifteen minutes after leaving Wally rolling in catnip, Dana turned off the main road into the long, tree-lined driveway of the resort that led to a huge front entrance reminiscent of the entrance to Jurassic Park in the movie.

Dana was certain that was the motif Gustavo Barca was going for, since fictional Jurassic Park was located in Costa Rica and a lot of tour operators and hotel owners tried to cash in on that tie-in, even though the movie was actually filmed in Hawaii.

She drove up to the guard station and stopped.

She'd been in the resort a few times, and they usually just gave a quick look at her and waved her through. It was a grand drive up to the posh resort, where the cheap villas started at $1,000 a night and where it wouldn't be uncommon to spot real

A-list stars and singers like Brittney Spears, Angelina Jolie, or George Clooney staying there.

She drove into the hotel's porte cochère, and a valet parked Big Red because she had no choice, since it seemed expensive hotels didn't like to have self-parking for its guests.

The valet attendants always smiled when they saw Big Red drive up. One young man had even professed that it was more fun to drive her iconic little red Jeep than the dime-a-dozen BMWs and Porsches he was accustomed to parking every day.

She walked inside to the front lobby and stopped. She had to give the devil, Gustavo Barca, his due. The resort was stunning. Shiny marble everywhere. So clean that you could eat off the floor.

Friendly staff members greeted you with every step you took. Okay, that part got on Dana's nerves right quick. *I can get from here to there without being asked ten times if I needed help.*

The one thing she found a bit off-putting with the decor Barca had chosen was that it was over the top and sliding into gaudy territory, and would fit in better on the Las Vegas Strip than in the lush, tropical forests in the mountains of Guanacaste.

The resort sat on five hectares of hillside gardens among lush tropical forests. The front lobby was wide open, with sweeping views of the jungle and the Pacific Ocean.

There were three pool areas, including an infinity pool that gave the illusion that the swimmer would tumble out of the water and down the mountain and into the Pacific Ocean.

Mother Nature had been cooperating again. Its skies were gray, but the sun kept peeking out from behind the clouds, and it was warm out. A nice day to lounge by the pool until the showers came.

The resort was busier than she expected for being midweek

during the wet season, but she figured most of the guests were with Donnelly's production company.

Okay, now what? Dana asked herself as she looked around. It wasn't like she could have the front desk people connect her to the room of Dakota, Arianna, and Robbie. She looked at her mobile phone, where she had the website for the show pulled up which showed the castaways for the upcoming season. It was like looking at a model agency's client roster. All the castaways were young and beautiful. She picked out Dakota whom met at the café and Robbie Gibbons from his fight with Rose Budd right away.

Robbie looked slightly different from what she had seen that night at the restaurant. He was drunk and disheveled on that night. On the website, he smiled wide, showing off his pearly whites with a mussed-up hairstyle which probably cost a fortune to make it look like it was messy and he didn't care. His eyes were so blue, they seemed to sparkle.

She hadn't met or seen Arianna Layton. She looked at her smiling photograph on the website.

Every single castaway on the website was beautiful. Perfect creatures made for TV.

Reality my foot, Dana thought. It was the myth that Hollywood loved to shove down regular people's throats about faces and bodies that most people could only dream to have.

It then dawned on her that Rose Budd's picture and profile were gone. She figured it made sense no matter how horrible it was what happened to her, since she wasn't going to be part of that season anymore. And she wondered if any of those other beautiful cast mates with million-dollar smiles were responsible for her death.

Aracelly Trejos had told Dana that the cast members hung out by the pool and that the infinity pool seemed to be the favorite spot for the beautiful people, so she made her way down the long steps that made their way from the front lobby down the hillside towards the pools.

She could see a smattering of beautiful people relaxing on teak chaise lounges with lush cushions and their own canopy tops.

Finding the people she was looking for seemed more difficult than she had thought, so she figured, what the heck, no time to be shy or prim and proper. She shouted out, "Dakota, Robbie, Arianna, are you guys out here?"

"Yeah, I'm here," Dana heard someone say. She turned towards the voice she had heard and she saw Dakota Hunter looking up at her from one of the chaise lounges.

"Hi, Dakota," Dana said, sounding excited. She was excited about having found her right away. She made her way towards her and she sat in a chair next to her without asking if she could join her.

"I've been looking for you," she said.

Dakota looked at her surprised, like she was trying to place her.

"You're the lady from the coffee shop."

"That's right."

She seemed disappointed.

"So, like, why are you looking for me?" she said dismissively as if she were talking to the hired help.

Dana bit her lip. "I wanted to ask you about what's been going with the show and with Rose Budd and TJ."

Dakota looked at her suspiciously. "You know what I know, lady, show is like shut down, we're all here wasting time waiting for the police to do whatever it is they're like doing, which is taking like forever. But at least I'm getting paid regardless to sit out here by this beautiful pool."

"Do you really think TJ killed her?"

"They did arrest him, so I guess so."

"You don't sound convinced."

"TJ was a bit of a slob, but he seemed like a nice guy. I know that Rose liked him. Not sure why. They were such an odd couple."

"So you knew they were seeing each other?"

"It seemed that way to me, but like suddenly she's like hooking up with Robbie and they're like always fighting and like bickering. They reminded me of my mom and dad, who were always at each other's throats. And then she like... died."

"Do you think Robbie could have hurt her?"

"I don't know. I think he was like all bark and no bite."

"Is he around?" Dana asked, looking around the pool area.

"No. He took Rose's death like really bad. He needed time to himself, so the producers said it was okay if he hung out by himself during the shutdown. Last I heard, he was camping down at the beach."

"At Mariposa Beach?"

Dakota looked at her like she had no clue what she had just said, so Dana added, "The little town down by the beach. Where my store is located."

She could almost hear Dakota's brain going *ding, ding, ding.* "Oh, yeah down there. That's where he's at. You guys have the best coffee and bagels. Even better than here at the resort."

"Thank you," Dana said, making a mental note to let Mindy and Leo know that her coffee and food had received a ringing endorsement over what an army of hoity-toity chefs were doing at the resort.

"Do you know where Arianna Layton is at?"

"Around here somewhere. Why?"

"I heard she didn't get along with Rose Budd."

"So you think she killed Rose," Dakota said, laughing.

"I just want to chat with her, is all."

"Arianna was my roomie on the island. She was with me

when Rose was killed, so you can cross her off your like suspect list, lady. Now, if you don't mind, I want to chill out before it rains."

Dana smiled and thanked Dakota for her help and made her way back out towards the front lobby. She figured it was more important for her to talk with Robbie Gibbons. And as much as she hated to agree with Dakota, it seemed like she could cross Arianna Layton from her list, since she seemed to have a solid alibi courtesy of Ms. Chill out over there.

TWENTY-EIGHT

Dana headed back down to Mariposa Beach. She parked on the street by the Qué Vista Restaurant and walked down to the beach.

She felt a couple raindrops on her arm. She looked up nervously but continued on looking for Robbie Gibbons.

She had been walking for a few minutes when she saw a small tent about five hundred yards away.

It was an orange-colored one-person tent that was pitched near the edge of the woods and the beach. It was a good spot to avoid the incoming tides pulling your stuff out to sea or at the very least flooding the tent.

She figured that had to be where Robbie was camping, since it wasn't common to see tents on the beach, so she changed course and began walking towards it.

She got closer and saw two people sitting in front of the tent. They were sitting right on the sand.

Dana recognized Robbie Gibbons, who was sitting cross-legged, looking out to the open water. He was shirtless and was wearing navy blue long boardshorts. Next to him was a woman leaning backwards, using her palms for support.

Robbie paid no attention as Dana got closer. He just kept looking at the water like he was meditating.

But the woman was looking right at her. By the time she was a few feet from them, she recognized the woman from the television show's website. It was Arianna Layton. Dana was close enough to see that Arianna was eyeballing her with contempt.

She was surprised to see her hanging out on the beach with Robbie. Adrianna stared Dana down the entire time with a scowl on her face that made Dana feel uncomfortable.

"Hi guys," Dana said casually as she reached them. She was trying to sound low-key and friendly.

Arianna seethed. "Dakota called me. She told us you were at the resort snooping around asking questions about us. Well, neither of us have anything to say to you, so take off."

Zing. She doesn't waste time, Dana thought.

"I'm just trying to help TJ before he's sent off to a horrible prison for something he didn't do. And don't you want Rose's real killer brought to justice?"

That seemed to break Robbie from his trance as he finally acknowledged her presence. He turned to look at her and said, "We do."

He sounded calm. Zen-like. The complete opposite of the brash, drunk, bro-like man she had first seen at the restaurant.

"So tell me what happened with Rose," Dana said.

"How are we supposed to know? That's what the police are doing. Do you think one of us killed Rose?" Arianna asked, sounding angry and defensive.

"Of course not," Dana said. But she was fibbing because she wasn't sure about anything anymore.

"Look. We've signed very strict contracts and confidential agreements with Russ Donnelly. He's made it very clear we are not to talk with anyone without the show, and he has an army of studio and private lawyers at his beck and call. So just go before you get us in a lot of legal trouble. Look what happened to TJ after he talked to you on the beach," Arianna said.

That took Dana aback. How could she make that big of a leap and blame her for the predicament TJ was in? She must have opened and shut her mouth at least three times, not knowing how to respond to that awful accusation, until Robbie spoke up.

"It's all right, Arianna, I don't care anymore."

"Babe, Russ can make your life a living nightmare," Arianna said. And for the first time since Dana arrived, Arianna sounded sweet, calm, and caring versus the acridness of her voice when she spoke to Dana. Then it registered to Dana. *Did she just call him babe?*

"You two... are together?"

"We love each other," Robbie said, smiling as he took Arianna's hand in his. Arianna smiled back.

"So everything has been a big act just like TJ said."

"There is very little reality in reality TV," Robbie replied.

He explained how Russ Donnelly was the puppet master behind the scenes. He decided who saw who on the show. So even though Rose Budd started seeing TJ and he and Arianna began to fall in love, that didn't matter to Russ Donnelly. He would pair up couples that would make for good ratings.

"It was in the contract that we all signed. Cast members couldn't date each other or anyone on the crew during the production of the show and for twelve months after the airing of the season finale," Arianna explained.

"So your relationships had to be kept secret," Dana said.

Robbie nodded his head. "Especially with TJ because he wasn't a cast member. Russ doesn't want anyone dating without his blessing, but he can make it work if cast mates date. But there is no angle he can use on the show if a cast member dates a crewmember. He called that a wasted relationship." Robbie sounded disgusted.

"We had to do what he wanted or he would kick us off the show, and crush us legally and financially," Arianna said.

"TJ didn't take being told he couldn't see Rose romantically too well. He was talking crazy, even wanted Rose to leave the show with him," Robbie said.

"Did Rose agree to that?"

"I don't know. One moment he had Rose agreeing to run off with him and to forget about the show, the next moment she was like, 'I can't. I have a contract. I want to be an actress and Russ can make sure that will never happen if I break my contract.'"

"Russ would also make sure TJ never worked at a Hollywood production again," Arianna added.

"So she stuck it out to be on the show?"

"Last I heard from her, she was thinking about quitting. She told me that she had enough dirt on Russ Donnelly that he would let her off her contract if she wanted," Arianna said.

"I doubt she had anything on him. She always got this sense of bravado when she drank. You saw how she can get," Robbie said.

Dana shrugged.

"So that was all show that night?"

"The date was and at first the fight was, but Rose drank way too much that night and she got way carried away. Russ was furious."

"He mentioned to us after you left that he was getting tired of her antics," Dana said, remembering back to that night. "Do you think Russ could have had something to do with her death?"

"I've thought about that, but I don't know. Rich, powerful men like Russ can get their way by destroying your life without having to take it."

"So what's next for you two?" Dana asked.

"Arianna and I both want off the show now after what happened to Rose, but Russ made it clear that nothing changes. As soon as the police allow it, we're back filming that flipping show. And we have no choice; he'll ruin us if we don't comply," Robbie said. He sounded dejected, beaten down by Hollywood.

Dana thanked them both and wished them luck as she began to walk back towards town on the beach. She felt bad for them. They were so young, with all these glamorous Hollywood dreams in their head, when the business reality of Hollywood could be a hideous thing.

Like a starstruck starlet getting off the bus in LA from small-town America with dreams of making it in Hollywood, only to fall prey to wolves and sharks.

Dana was convinced that there was no way Robbie and Arianna had anything to do with Rose's death. They were sweet, confused kids playing roles of brash, out-of-control cast-aways for the television show.

As Dana walked back to town, she had plenty of thoughts going through her head about TJ. Could she have been wrong about him all along? Maybe he became mad with Rose for not standing up to Russ Donnelly. Maybe he became so mad that she chose the show and her Hollywood dreams over him. But then again TJ insisted they were keeping the romance secret because he didn't want to get blacklisted by Russ Donnelly. Heck, he even took back what he had told Dana and Benny that night on the beach. So he sure as heck didn't seem to stand up to Russ Donnelly.

She had gotten about fifty feet away from where Robbie and Arianna were camping, still lost in her thoughts, when she saw a black car driving on the beach, heading her way. It closed in fast, and she could tell it was the Range Rover that Russ Donnelly was chauffeured around town in.

The Range Rover stopped right in front of Dana, making her take a step back, fearing it would run her over.

Russ Donnelly got out of the backseat. Henry Robertson, the assistant producer got out from the driver's side.

Russ Donnelly walked towards Dana aggressively, making her nervous. She looked back, and she wasn't too far from Robbie and Arianna if she needed to run for help. Henry Robertson walked a few steps behind Donnelly.

"This needs to stop, Ms. Kirkpatrick," Donnelly said, walking up to her. He stopped right in front of her as if to block her path. Henry stood behind him, looking down at his feet.

"What are you talking about?"

"You can't be harassing my employees."

"Excuse me?"

"First you go talk to TJ in jail. Now I find out you were at the resort talking with Dakota, and now I catch you out here bugging Robbie and Arianna."

"So what? You don't own the resort. And down here on the beach is public property. I can walk to and talk to whomever I want. And at least I visited TJ. You just washed your hands of him, not even getting him a decent lawyer."

His eyes got big and his nostrils flared. She could tell he wasn't a man used to being talked to that way, especially by a woman commoner.

"These are my people. They work for me. They've signed contracts with me. I own them for the next two years. You can't talk to them. Period. And I'll let you know that Detective Picado is livid about your talking to his prisoner behind his back."

"Behind his back? You're both delusional. The police told me it was up to TJ if he wanted to talk to me, and he did, so they let me in. I did nothing wrong. And you don't own any of these people. They might work for you, but that's it. If Robbie wants to talk to me on the public beach, so be it."

"I have iron-clad contracts with all of them. I dictate who they can talk to and who they can't, and I'll be making it crystal clear to everyone on the show that they can no longer talk to you, even to say hello. They will be fired and I will enforce the financial penalties of their signed agreements with me."

Dana was stunned at the audacity, but Russ Donnelly wasn't finished.

"You see, I tell them what they can wear and what they can't wear. I control what they eat. How they must behave. I even control whom they can date. So until the contract expires, I own them, missy."

"You have some nerve and some ego on you," Dana said. "Well, I didn't sign your contract or that stupid NDA you wanted me to sign, meaning I can talk to whoever I please, so go jump in that water," Dana said, pointing at the ocean.

Out of the blue, Henry Robertson, who had been standing behind Russ Donnelly quietly and meekly, erupted like a dormant volcano.

"Don't you talk to him that way! He's Russ Donnelly!" he shouted at the top of his lungs. It was such a sudden outburst and so loud that both Donnelly and Dana flinched. She looked back towards the tent and saw Robbie and Arianna getting up. No doubt they heard Henry shouting.

She turned back to look at Henry, whose face was red with anger. It surprised her, since she had even forgotten he had been standing there behind Donnelly. His whole body demeanor had changed. His eyes had grown wide and his nostrils flared even more than Russ Donnelly's had as he made his way from standing behind Donnelly to stand in front of him, as if to protect him from Dana.

He continued seething. "You talk to Mr. Donnelly with respect." He pointed his finger at Dana's face. "He's a very important and powerful man. Don't you forget that."

Donnelly seemed taken aback at Henry's outburst and threatening body language. He stepped in front of Henry and put his hand on his chest, as if to push him to go back to stand behind him quietly as before.

"Okay, okay, we've all lost our tempers here. Let's let cooler heads prevail," Donnelly said, holding both his hands in the air. "I apologize for my behavior, Ms. Kirkpatrick, and that of my assistant. I have nothing more to say to you. My attorney will be in touch. Have a good day."

Just like that, the whole tense exchange was over. Diffused by Donnelly himself. He and Henry got back into the Range Rover, which did a U-turn, and head back into town.

Dana stood there, stunned.

TWENTY-NINE

It had been such a crazy week for Dana. Benny would head
back to town on Friday night, and she couldn't wait. She had
told him everything that had gone down on the beach with Russ
Donnelly and his raging assistant when they FaceTimed that
evening.

"It's just a bunch of hot air from a man who's used to always
getting his way," Benny had told her. "And if a lawyer contacts
you, just tell them they need to talk to your lawyer and give
them my number. Do not say anything else but that to them."

Dana agreed and thanked him.

She went to bed early that night, much to Wally's delight,
who was no longer buzzing from catnip and was ready to crash,
so he had already claimed half the bed as his.

She climbed under the covers as the kitty purred. After a
moment, Wally got up, stretched, and jumped onto her chest,
going nose to nose with Dana as he purred loudly.

"I guess I can't go to bed if I don't give you some attention
first," Dana said, petting the top of his white head and
scratching his chin and the back of his ears. She drifted to sleep
petting Wally.

She woke up at six o'clock a.m. She looked around and Wally was MIA as he sometimes did. She yawned and got out of bed.

She would go on that run on the beach that she had been avoiding for days.

It had been her favorite running route until she had found Rose Budd's body, and she hadn't been back there since then.

Now things were falling into place. Benny had come through and found TJ a top-notch attorney who had agreed to represent him, so at the very least he would get decent legal representation.

As far as she was concerned, there wasn't anything else she could do. She would let the lawyers handle it. She had given herself way too much credit as being some detective, and all she had done was get everyone and their brother mad at her.

It really wasn't any of her business, she thought as she put on her running gear. She looked out the window and the sun was slowly making its way up into the sky.

Mother Nature had dumped enough rain during the night to make Moses nervous. She figured Mother Nature would spare them from another deluge until the afternoon.

Dana stretched for ten minutes. She had noticed the older she got, the more important it was to stretch before doing anything strenuous to her body.

She was all set by 6:20 a.m. She made her way outside and out her side door, which spilled out onto the footpath. She usually began her run with a walk to the beach, but she felt like she had a lot of energy pinned up, so she began running right out of the gate, making her way through the woods and down towards the beach. She was keeping up a good pace as she made it down to an empty Main Street. She ran down the street past the Ark Row shops. The town was quiet and desolate that early except for Leo Salas, who was making his way towards the cafe to get ready for the morning crowd seeking coffee and bagels. Dana waved to him. He smiled and waved back. She figured Mindy was around somewhere but didn't see her.

She picked up the pace as she continued running past the Qué Vista Restaurant and then onto the beach, where she picked up the pace, running on the wet hard sand until she reached the rock formation. The end of the road. The point where she had to turn back. The spot where she had found Rose Budd's body.

She stopped, breathing heavily. She stood there looking at the rocks, expecting to see the body still there. She trembled at the thought.

It was one of the main reasons she had chosen that route. She had avoided the spot like the plague. But it was time for her to confront her fears. She had found a dead body there. But she couldn't let that keep her away from her regular life. She had to put the tragedy into the right focus to be respectful without letting it loom over her life with negativity.

So she looked at the spot for a little longer. She said a quick prayer for Rose Budd, praying that her killer would be brought to justice even if it really was TJ.

After another moment of silence, she turned to run back to town and saw a figure walking on the beach towards her. She couldn't make out who it was, and usually it wouldn't concern her, since there were always people on the beach going for an early-morning run or walk like she was doing, but there might be a killer out there on the loose. She hadn't thought things through.

She started running again but the man waved at her, so she waved back, not knowing yet who he was, but it seemed he knew who she was.

They were both heading towards each other, and he finally

approached her close enough for her to make out who he was. She stopped. It was Henry Robertson who had gotten so angry with her yesterday. He was walking towards her.

"Hi there," he yelled out at her, as he was close enough to hear.

She felt awkward running into him after yesterday's confrontation and wasn't too keen on talking to him, but she bade him good morning.

Dana thought perhaps he wanted to apologize for losing his cool yesterday.

Then she noticed he was wearing a shower cap underneath a baseball cap and a tracksuit with gloves on.

"Beautiful morning," he said nonchalantly.

He was now right in front of her.

Dana noticed his face turn dark. His eyes were black like charcoal. *Have they always been that ominous?* she thought.

"Well, I'm off to finish my run," Dana said as she started up again.

And he just pounced.

"You're not going anywhere, missy," he said, seething as he grabbed her wrist then with his other hand he shoved her down to the ground while still holding on to her wrist. He was six feet tall and outweighed her by at least one hundred pounds.

Dana tumbled onto the ground hard. She yelped. "What are you doing," she screamed, but he said nothing as he grabbed her by the hair and began to drag her on the sand towards the rocks.

"Let go of me," Dana shouted as she struggled to get out of his hold. She was trying to reach her hands up towards him but was just punching air. She kicked hard but was kicking up sand. She was surprised how strong he was. He seemed so meek and soft-spoken before, so he didn't really radiate the strength he possessed.

"Shut up," he said as he kept dragging her towards the rocks and out of view from the main drag of the beach.

"What are you doing?" Dana cried.

"What do you think?" He sounded cruel.

"But why?"

"Because you keep sticking your nose into my father's business."

"What? I don't even know who your father is. Please, let me go," Dana pleaded.

"Russ Donnelly is my father, and I'm making sure trouble-makers like you and Rose Budd don't hurt him."

"You?"

He laughed. "You catch on quick."

"He's... he's your father?"

Henry nodded, his grip on her getting stronger.

"Don't do your father's evil bidding, Henry, walk away, you're young."

He laughed.

"He doesn't know I'm going to kill you. He would be furious. Just like he was when he found out I killed Rose Budd. He got so mad at me because he had to clean up my mess by framing that idiot TJ."

"Why?" Dana asked. She was now crying.

"I overheard Rose and TJ talking. She wanted off the show and so did TJ. They said they had enough behind-the-scenes dirt on the show that my dad would have no choice but to let them off their contract and pay them a bunch of money to keep quiet about it. Can you believe that? They wanted to blackmail my dad so they could run off and be together. After everything he had done for them. He was going to make Rose a star, and she wanted to throw that away to be with that disgusting slob, TJ," Henry said incredulously.

"Don't do this, Henry." Dana pleaded for her life.

He looked around and felt he had enough cover from the rocks, so he let go of her and shoved her onto the sand, holding her down on the ground with his right knee and left forearm. She tried to wiggle loose, but he had her pinned down to the ground hard. She could barely wiggle her upper body, so all she could do was kick her feet wildly, to no avail. She began to scream, but she knew no one in town could hear her.

Henry must have known that too, because he smirked and then he picked up a rock that was lying on the sand. It was the size of a softball, hard and rugged. She cried and begged him not to do it as he held the rock up over his head. She could sense his hate boring into her and she could feel the cool splash back from the waves on her face, which remarkably calmed her down a bit.

"This is your fault, you should have minded your own business," he said, seething as he began to bring the rock down towards her face. She closed her eyes and prayed, and suddenly she heard a horn blaring wildly in the distance.

She opened her eyes, and she could see through her tears that Henry was distracted, looking towards the sound of the blaring horn. He had brought the rock down and loosened his hold of her as his attention was on the sound of an approaching vehicle that continued to blow its horn. He wasn't looking at her, so she caught him off guard and shoved him, and using her legs for leverage, she flipped him off of her and he toppled onto the sand. Dana jumped to her feet and took off running, jumping rocks like she was Lolo Jones clearing hurdles.

She ran towards the vehicle that continued honking and flicking its lights on and off. It was a black Range Rover that stopped near the rocks. Dana ran to it and saw Russ Donnelly get out of the driver's side. She stopped short and began to walk back away from him.

"Are you okay?" Donnelly asked, sounding frightened.

"No, thanks to your crazy son back there. He tried to kill me. He killed Rose."

She had gone from petrified to plain scared to angry. She turned back towards the rocks to make sure Henry wasn't coming after her, but he wasn't. She then turned her attention back towards Donnelly and made her way to the other side of the Range Rover, using it as a buffer zone between her and Donnelly and his deranged son.

"He's not well," Donnelly said.

"No kidding. That's the understatement of the decade."

"Please, I'll give you one million dollars. Cash. If we can keep this between us."

"No way." Dana was now in full anger mode.

"Two million dollars. I'll make sure he gets the help he needs, so he doesn't hurt anyone else. What happened with Rose, it was an accident. He didn't mean to do it."

"Oh, yes, I did," Henry yelled as he made his way down from the rocks.

"Shut up, Henry," Donnelly said.

"She was talking trash about my Dad, as usual. And she was doing it so nonchalantly, without a care in the world as she was painting her nails in a garish bright orange color. She didn't know he was my dad, so she kept saying how she would ruin him if he didn't let her off the show. I tried to keep quiet. I even closed my eyes to do my breathing exercise, but she wouldn't shut up. When I opened my eyes, she was on the floor and I was holding a bloody fire extinguisher in my hands."

"It was an accident. He needs help," Donnelly said.

Dana couldn't believe what she had just heard, her face ashen.

"Come on now, three million dollars. Don't be foolish. You can't walk away from three million dollars, cash."

"Watch me," Dana said as she took off running back towards town.

She looked back and she could see Russ Donnelly physically restraining his son from chasing after her. That sight gave her an adrenaline boost as she ran even faster than she could usually muster back into town.

EPILOGUE

The next few days were a whirlwind of activity. Dana was able to make it back to town safely and in record time.

She ran into Books, Bagels, and Lattes, where Mindy and Leo were getting ready to open up for the day.

She hadn't realized what a mess she was until she saw the shock and fear in Mindy and Leo's eyes.

"What happened to you?" Mindy had asked with tears welling in her eyes.

Dana looked in the mirror, realizing she looked like a walking horror show. She was drenched in sweat and water from the waves. The back of her hair was a matted clump of wet sand. Her clothing was disheveled, and she had bruises on her wrists and arm. She would later find out she had an even bigger bruise on her chest from Henry Robertson kneeling into her to pin her into the ground.

They called the police. Detectives Picado and Rojas were staying at a hotel in Playa Guiones, but they made the fifteen-minute trip in about ten minutes flat. They even beat officer Freddy Sanchez into town as he came roaring on his motorcycle.

Dana told them what happened. Officer Freddy radioed for

police backup as Picado and Rojas jumped in their car and sped down to where Dana had told him Henry Robertson had attacked her.

Dana would later find out that the detectives got there too late. Russ Donnelly and Henry Robertson were long gone.

Picado put out an APB on a black Range Rover and on Russ Donnelly and Henry Robertson.

Eventually Picado and Rojas tracked them down to a small private airport near the Tranquil Bay Resort that was owned by Gustavo Barca and used by the richest of his guests to fly into the peninsula on their own private jets and helicopters.

Donnelly's private jet had been parked there since he arrived to town. An airport employee told the police that they had missed Donnelly and Robertson by just a few minutes. They had arrived in a rush and were in the air in mere minutes.

Picado was beside himself with anger. He would later drag Barca through the mud for allowing a murder suspect to escape, but Barca claimed neither he nor his private airport employees had any idea the police wanted them.

Dana didn't care much for Barca, but she believed him. How would he have known that Donnelly and his son were trying to escape arrest? She figured they were in the air in less than thirty minutes after Henry Robertson had attacked her.

Donnelly always flew in his own Gulfstream G650 private jet that he always had on standby. The two of them must have driven straight from the spot where Henry tried to kill Dana to the airport in mere minutes, and from there they were up in the air right away.

But Picado wouldn't let them slip away. He immediately issued a Red Notice with Interpol on Russ Donnelly and Henry Robertson that meant they were wanted persons for prosecution and should be immediately arrested if found. He also alerted the FBI, which put alerts on all the municipal airports in Southern California.

By the time Donnelly's jet landed at the Van Nuys Airport near Los Angeles, the LAPD and the FBI were there to greet them.

Dana was amazed at the hoopla that followed. To say that the case made international headlines was like saying there was a little fire on the Hindenburg.

You had the celebrity factor. Even though these were D-list reality TV celebrities, still it had the Hollywood allure to it, so the public's hunger for any information on the case was insatiable, and the media was more than happy to give its hungry audiences fodder to gorge themselves on.

As hectic as things had gotten at Mariposa Beach when the production company arrived in town, it was nothing compared to the second wave of the media invasion.

ABC. NBC. CBS. FOX. CNN. TMZ. It seemed like every three-lettered news network was in town, covering the story. The local news outlets and bloggers were all over the story.

Dana had to hide out at Casa Verde, grateful for her home's big front gates and high-definition video security cameras that kept reporters and their ambitious cameramen from misbehaving too much.

A few months later, once she became yesterday's news, they finally left her alone.

Soon after that, all the true crime programs did their own program on the case, including *Dateline*, 20/20, and two shows on Investigation Discovery. Dana felt the actress portraying her on Investigation Discovery did the best job, and was excited that Keith Morrison handled her story on *Dateline*, even though she thought the actress portraying her was about a hundred times prettier than she was, to which Benny said, "Pish." He was so sweet.

As if things weren't whacky enough during that time, Costa Rica and the United States got into a little jurisdiction back-and-forth over which country could prosecute Henry Robertson.

In the end, the Costa Rican government decided they didn't want to spend the money and time to extradite Henry Robertson back to Costa Rica, so they washed their hands of the killer.

They denied Henry bail, so he remained in the LAPD lockup. It took months, but they finally charged Henry Robertson for the murder of Denise Budd. That's when Dana found out Rose Budd had been her stage name. Denise Budd came from a small Ohio town and moved to LA to make it in the show business as Rose Budd, only to lose her life at the hands of Henry Robertson. And for what? It angered Dana to think about it.

A lot more came out about Henry Robertson and Russ Donnelly's relationship after he was arrested and charged.

Henry was the illegitimate son of Russ Donnelly. His mother had been one of Russ Donnelly's many mistresses. Donnelly kept his identity a secret because he didn't want to go through a fourth very expensive divorce.

Donnelly supported Henry and his mother while he grew up, but he wasn't involved in his life. Henry's mother would tell him all about his famous father, and they enjoyed watching *The Island* on TV. When Henry graduated from college, he came looking for his father, and the two reconnected. Russ Donnelly had three daughters, but Henry was his only son, so he took him under his wing and gave him a job as an assistant producer for his company, but their true relationship was hidden from everyone and didn't come out until their arrest.

Henry Robertson had some anger-management problems in his past—that did not surprise Dana. He went from cold to hot in a nanosecond and didn't think of the consequences of losing his temper and lashing out.

He claimed he didn't mean to kill Rose Budd. He tried to talk her out of embarrassing his father, and when she refused, he just snapped and struck her with the fire extinguisher. When he realized what he had done, he panicked, and tossed her body into the water, hoping it would never be found, but the tides didn't want to be complicit in his murder, so instead of taking her out to sea, they brought Rose's body to the shore and onto those rocks where Dana found her early the next morning.

When Russ Donnelly found out what his son had done, he framed the murder on TJ and used his money and power to cover it all up.

He too was charged with a litany of crimes.

Donnelly had enough money that it might be years before the case went to court, and could easily pay the $1,000,000 bond to get out of jail so he could wait for the trial in his Beverly Hills mansion.

Donnelly made the media rounds to apologize for what his son had done, but he said his son was insane, therefore he didn't know what he was doing when he killed Rose Budd. He was angling for a not guilty because of mental illness.

That sounded like a bunch of hogwash to Dana. Henry seemed like he knew what he was doing when he tried to kill her, so it seemed it was just legal mumbo jumbo to get his son out of prison.

One thing that Donnelly could no longer avoid was divorce

number four in the communal property land that is California. His wife would get half the marital assets. *Good for her*, Dana thought.

The Island reality television show also didn't make it. The bad behavior of Donnelly off and on the set came to light.

Stories surfaced that he was a bully, running the set like a dictator. His employees and former castaways began to come forward with their own horror stories.

Also coming to light was the sexual harassment inflicted on just about every woman by not only Russ Donnelly but also the show's popular host, Chris Day.

In the era of #metoo, his fall from show business grace was swift and fast. He was finished. The network fired Chris Day and Russ Donnelly and they canceled the hit reality show.

The cast members went back to their normal lives without being able to finish recording the show. Dana figured most would be very upset about that, but not TJ Summers, Robbie Gibbons, and Arianna Layton. They were free of Russ Donnelly. *Good for them*, Dana thought.

Speaking of TJ, they freed him from jail in Nicoya right after the truth came out about Henry killing Rose.

He called Dana to thank her on his way to the airport. He told her that Picado even shook his hand and apologized.

TJ told her he would love to give her a hug for her help, but he was too scared to stick around the country in case they changed their mind and arrested him again, so he took an Uber from the police station straight to the airport in Liberia and took the first flight back to the States, almost maxing out his credit card.

He would later send Dana a handwritten note and a beautiful flower arrangement, thanking her. It surprised her he was so insightful and proper. It was a side she hadn't seen before, since he was mostly unwashed, uncouth, and drunk around town. But the despair he was dealing with after Rose's murder was probably to blame for that side to him. The thoughtful, caring man that sent Dana the letter and flowers must have been the real TJ and the man Rose had fallen for.

He told her he was still planning to work for the industry, but he was moving to Atlanta, where the entertainment business was booming. He told her he liked that the Atlanta entertainment industry was a little removed from the plasticity of Hollywood and LA.

Last Dana heard from TJ was when he sent her an email to let her know he was doing well and that he was in TV heaven, having been hired as a prop guy for the *Walking Dead* TV series.

Dana recovered from the wounds Henry Robertson inflicted on her physically and emotionally. She wouldn't let him take an iota of her joy of life from her.

She was glad that Rose's killer was caught and would probably spend the rest of his life in prison, and that TJ was vindicated and doing well.

Russ Donnelly's fall from grace in the entertainment world and his own legal woes seemed a fair comeuppance as far as Dana was concerned.

The media frenzy came and went, and once again the small beach town began to go back to normal.

Books, Bagels, and Lattes continued going strong. Dana and Benny enjoyed the peace and quiet before the wet season bit the dustbin allowing the dry season to come out of its hibernation, bringing with it a horde of money-spending tourists to her small and sleepy slice of tropical paradise known as Mariposa Beach.

WHAT'S NEXT?

A rare orchid is discovered growing in a private reserve near Mariposa Beach. Murder and Mayhem ensues and Dana Kirkpatrick is sucked into the middle of a murder mystery, again!

An Orchid To Die For will be published in December of 2019!

ABOUT K.C.

I was born and raised in Costa Rica, but now live in San Francisco, California. I've always loved cozy mysteries, so when I decided to write one, I just knew I had to base it in my home country of Costa Rica!

That's how this beach cozy mystery series came about. I'm excited to bring you more cozy mysteries set in the beautiful tropical Pacific Coast of Costa Rica.

You can learn more about me and my books over at my website: www.KCAmes.com.

Sign up for my newsletter for book updates, animal pics, and my recipe book of traditional Costa Rica dishes, for free:

kcames.com/subscribe

And join my reader group on Facebook to say hello and make new friends:

kcames.com/group

ALSO BY K.C. AMES

A Beach House To Die For

A Book To Die For

A Reality Show To Die For